UNDYING LUST

A NOVEL BY

SIR PATRICK BIJOU

Other Novels by Sir Patrick Bijou

- Karmic Love
- Beginners of Nowhere
- Undercover

BOOK DESCRIPTION

Vivienne is a hardworking young lady in her twenties who loves to take control of her life and provide solutions to a problem that comes her way at work and even in her private life. She has everything she wanted, but one thing is missing; love (a sexual experience).

She is however lusting after her dad's mechanic, Danny, whom her dad puts in charge to look after her. He's way older than her, but she likes it so, she hates going out with younger guys or guys her age.

She's on a quest to make Danny feel the same way she's feeling, but it seems quite herculean.

Will she ever succeed and make him feel the same way she's feeling for him?

ABOUT THE AUTHOR

Sir Patrick is a dynamic Investment banker, Fund Manager, and JUDGE for the International Court of Justice and International Criminal Courts, he is also a published Author. Sir Patrick's journey into content writing has allowed him to become an exceptionally motivated and enthusiastic author and professional communicator. Experienced in both proactive campaign-driven and responsive communications.

He lives and writes from the United Kingdom and is the author of several books in finance and fiction, UNDYING LOVE is his fourth novel.

CONTENTS

CHAPTER ONE

I can count the number of guys I've slept with on one hand. I can count the number of guys I've wanted to sleep with on one finger. Moreover, that man is on his way to my apartment right now. However, if I end up having sex with Danny tonight, I have my dad to thank or blame, and it depends on how this goes.

It's 4:05 in the evening and the chime on my electronic meat thermometer dings and alerts me. Perfect. Danny will be here at 4:15 pm so that gives the roast beef ten minutes to rest before I need to serve it. I do another walk through my tiny apartment for a final confirmation of the details of my plan of seduction.

Pecan pie warming on the stove top and combining with the roast for the perfect scent—check.

Tools necessary for removing and storing the window A/C unit lying next to it—check.

Pristine linen sheets replaced with Walmart cheepie sheets that I am willing to have sex on—check.

My heart is racing a little, ten years of anticipation will do that to you. I have myself checked in the full-length mirror in my bedroom one more time. Even I have to admit, I've nailed this outfit. My new jeans keep it casual but have strategically placed seems and fading to highlight all my curves. My ass could turn me on in these. My tee shirt looks like I just threw it on, but I shopped for an hour online for this specific one—it's a little sheer, hangs off one shoulder, and highlights the blue lacy bra underneath. My toes are freezing on the hardwood floor, but the cold can't stop me from being barefoot just to show off my shell-pink pedi—my feet are one of my best features; no way I'm hiding them today. If all goes as planned, I can warm them under Danny's gorgeous muscular legs during our postsex snuggle

I grab the tousle spray from the bathroom cabinet and primp my perfectly- styled messy beach waves one last time. I wish you luck in trying to resist me, Danny, you're going to need it.

At 4:15 pm I hear the buzzer from the building's front door announcing his punctual arrival. I knew it; Danny doesn't do lateness. He was never late one day in the eight years that my dad was his boss. Yes, his reliability is one of the reasons I crave this man. I buzz him in and use the two minutes it will take him to climb the stairs to my apartment to pull the roast from the oven and tent it with the waiting piece of foil.

I try to suppress my smile as I open the door. I'm keeping it casual like he's just Danny moving my air conditioner to storage, not my undying crush finally ready for me.

He is definitely looking laid back, leaning on the door frame, hands in his jean's pockets, looking at the floor. He looks up and stares at me, shifting the toothpick to the other side of his mouth, drawing my attention (once again) to how damn full his lips are. I swear I'm turned on even when he hasn't said a word.

Then he says. —Roast?

I regain my composure and nod. —Yep.

He takes a deep breath and launches himself off the door frame. — Pecan pie too?

—Yep.

And he lets out a long frustrated sigh. What? NO! Not this. Not again.

He walks over to the window and starts to pull the air conditioner from its perch. It's wedged tightly into the ancient window frame and puts up a fight. In my mind, I appreciate it for making this harder for him. In muted distress, I watch him as he takes a screwdriver from my toolkit and uses it to push the frame back where it has embedded itself into the unit. After replacing the screwdriver in its correct slot (Do you see why he is perfect for me?), he shifts his weight back, stretches his exquisitely muscular arms around the machine and heaves. I can't help but swoon a little at the way his shoulder muscles flex a n d settle as he leans the old hundred-plus pound thing against his chest.

He looks at me, but only to get my attention, then nods toward the door.

Let's go.

I put up a weak smile which can't hide my disappointment. Sure, he might've seen that I anticipated and wanted more.

I open the door to my apartment then walk ahead of him down the three flights of steps to the basement storage area. He's quiet; not even trying to make small talks like asking about my job or my new car. This isn't what I had envisioned; this is worst than my expectations.

I admit I knew there was a chance he would turn me down, but I weighted it as a slight chance. He could still be getting over his divorce, but it's been over a year she left him. How long can he mourn the loss of the stupid, wussy woman? I've written off his reluctance to let her go when she has their son. That's the only reason I can see for him not moving on to someone better, someone who won't bail at the first sign of trouble, someone with a backbone— Someone like me.

The padlock on the door of my storage locker is giving me little trouble as I fumble with it. I probably should have had it unlocked already so he wouldn't have to stand there holding the A/C unit, but I didn't want to leave it unlocked for too long, and I did not plan on him doing this right away. My roast and pie were supposed to work their magic and slow this project down so it would last until morning, or at least a few hours.

Finally, the lock opens, I open the door and step aside for him to enter the tiny room. I fight the urge to lock him in there and hold him until he wakes up and notices what is right in front of him.

I didn't ask you to do this, you know.

He sets the unit down with a grunt and turns to me, —I know. He dust off his hands and walks past me as I shut and lock the door.

I'd already made a deal with the maintenance guy to do this for me.

He starts back up the stairs ahead of me, —Yeah, well your dad asked me to come over here and do this, so here I am. You're welcome.

Damn it. I did sound ungrateful, but this was about so much more than the air conditioner. —I made you dinner to thank you.

He doesn't say a word in response to that.

We reached the landing with the building's front door and he turns toward it. I can't let him go yet. —You're not staying for dinner?

Can't. I've got to go to work.

Oh, puhleeese, what a lame bull-shit lie. I know where he works, I know his hours, and I know that he doesn't have to go back to work tonight. His shift ended at three and he's not wearing his work uniform. —Did you change shifts?

No, but I've got to go. He makes a move for the door and I block him.

My anger and embarrassment has me at a loss for words. I open my mouth to speak, but I'm afraid of what might come out. I need time to process this and formulate a response. For once, I have no plan B because I didn't plan on failing this spectacularly. All I can think to do is kill him with kindness.

Take the pie at least. I can wrap it up and you can share it with the other guys on your crew.

No, not tonight. He moves toward the door again, I block him once more.

Danny, I...

Vivey, I told your dad I would come over here and help you move your air conditioner. That's all he asked me to do and that's all I'm going to do. He reaches out and touches my arm as if the contact will somehow lessen the blow. —I., He checks his watch. —I gotta go. I'm gonna be late.

He pushes past me, his size and warmth momentarily engulfing me, his Irish Spring scent lingering in his wake as he passes by. He doesn't look back as he descended the stairs then gets on a motorcycle illegally parked on the sidewalk.

When did he get a motorcycle? He guns the engine, checks for pedestrians and cars and pulls out onto Drayton Street heading toward downtown.

I'm not sure how long I stand there, recovering from the shock of that short, excruciating brush-off. I had an armoury of temptation ready in my apartment, and he ran after he caught a whiff of my first shot. I shut the door tightly and check that the handle has locked. I love this apartment and this neighborhood, they are good and kind of peaceful, but I'm not naive enough to not be aware of its dangers.

On my way up the stairs, I pull my phone from my back pocket to call Dom who's on standby, waiting for her BFF sex summary. She answers, —So soon? Jeez, he's quick on the draw!

CHAPTER TWO

There wasn't any draw, best friend, he moved the air conditioner then practically sprinted out of here. I reply to her, plop down on the couch and hug my favorite pink chenille pillow to my chest. It's like putting a fluffy Band-aid over where I hurt.

So start from the beginning, he got there and then what happened?

A Dom-analysis could take an hour, five times longer than the actual date and I'm not up for it. —I don't know. He got here, smelled the roast and pie, asked me if that's what he smelled, then immediately started pulling the air conditioner out of the window. He was definitely on a mission to get the hell out of here. He even lied, said he had to go back to work and he wasn't even wearing a uniform. I mean, what the hell, like I'm not going to notice that?

That shuts Dom up. Danny is not known for lying if anything he could be called too blunt, honest to a fault.

I need an exorcism, Dom, I need to purge him from my soul.

I won't argue with you there, friend, I've been listening to you moan and drool over him for ten.

I know, I know. I cut her off because I don't want a review of all the stupid ways I've embarrassed myself over Danny. —Cut me some slacks. I was fifteen.

Ok, when you met him, but this past year...V, if he hasn't made a move by now. I can tell she doesn't want to say it and hurt my feelings and she doesn't have to.

He isn't going to. Ouch, that hurts to say, but it's like ripping off a Band-aid. I need to do it. I need to move on. —Just give me sometime.

Sure, yeah I know. A sad silence hangs heavy between us because of only

Dom knows how hard this will be for me.

You and mama going to play bingo tonight? I change the subject. I know they are. Dom and her mama and her aunties all play bingo together every Thursday night at their church. —How goes the wedding fund?

They are all pooling their winnings and saving up for Dom's wedding.

It's growing, baby, it's growing. Luis's aunt and grandma are going in with us now.

Dom's family is the opposite of mine, huge and involved while mine's small and distant. Dom still lives with her mama and siblings and will until she

you want to come with us tonight? She asks me, — the girls will make you feel better. We'll down a few cervezas.

No, not tonight and besides, I'm an Irish girl... I've got to drown my sorrows in whiskey. I think it's required.

All right, you have the night off to drown your sorrows.

Thanks, Dom, and thanks also for understanding.

Hey, I get it. Believe me I've been there the whole time. The man's smile and body alone could make any girl fantasise getting laid with him. Moreover, he used to be really sweet to you. Ever since your dad moved away and his divorce, he's changed.

Yeah, he has. I guess he's only nice to me because of my dad. Now that he's not here.

Are you going to tell your dad to stop sending him over to help you? She asks, —you know he'll do it again.

Damn, she's right! It's a losing battle with my dad to convince him to let me take care of myself. I have spent half my life taking care of him, and me, and our house, and he still treats me like I'm a child.

No! Oh hell, you're right. If this weren't the most perfect effing apartment in this city, I would move my ass to Sweden and get away from both of them.

Dom laughs, —Then Big Mike would find some dude named Sven and have him at your place taking care of you.

As long as Sven isn't frigid, I say and we both laugh out loud at that. Do you think that's it. Dom asks, — Do you think Danny's frigid?

Oh, hell no! Like I've always said, there is something about the way he moves, still can't put my finger on it, but there's something in his stride that tells me he'd be a really great lay.

No, don't go there, my friend, assume he's a horrible lay and really shitty kisser.

With those lips?

Even Dom can't argue with that. —Ok, so he might be a good kisser, but he doesn't deserve you.

Because...?

Because he is a estúpido, a box of rocks. Come on V, how can he not see by now what an amazing catch you are? You are smart, successful, a gourmet cook, totally cute and if he ever gave you the chance, I'm sure you would wear him out in bed until he died a happy man.

I would rock his world!

Save that for someone who deserves it.

Like who, Dom? In twenty-five years, I have met only one man, one, who meets my standards.

And don't you dare lower them now.

I'm going to die alone as a cat lady, still looking for that perfect guy.

No you're not. There is going to be a guy who appreciates how hard you work to make everything perfect. Did you pour yourself that drink yet?

I put my phone on speaker and set it on the bar cart in the corner of the living room.

Pouring it now, I say to her. She can hear me put ice in a tumbler and pour Jameson over it.

Of course, you had ice in the bucket.

And little lemon wedges too. I add one to my drink and pour water from the pitcher.

What are you going to do now? Dom asks, playing the mother hen role like she is used to, just like her mom. Both of them have taken up the job to be the mother I lost ever since my mom died.

Cut the roast into sandwich meat so I can take it to some guys who will appreciate it.

Ok, good. No single ones yet?

Dom is always pushing me to find romance at work which, number one, goes against my policy of never dating at work, and two, she doesn't know these guys like I do. They are salesmen, always polite and kind and joking and so full of shit it practically leaks out their ears.

No single ones.

At least Bob appreciates you.

Indeed Bob does appreciate me. He's my boss, Bob Brockhaus, the lead salesman in international sales for JetStream Aerospace. He travels the world selling private jets to billionaires, and he does a damn good job of it, in significant part because he has me. I make his chaotic home and work life run like a well-oiled machine, and he makes sure I am paid well to do that. Indeed, I have Bob.

CHAPTER THREE

I've put the guys who work in the sales department into three categories: DAL Divorced and looking, DAG — Divorced and gave up, and MAH — Married and hanging on by a thread. International sales (or I-sales to insiders) sounds cool and sexy and from the outside might look cool and sexy, but it's a lifestyle that is hell on a marriage.

Right now my boss, Bob, is in Dubai. He's there at least once or twice a month and stays a few days each time. After three days home, he'll be flying to Hong Kong. From there, he will fly to Melbourne, and then Seoul before coming home for another three days. He's married, again. Her name is Kara, and she is wife number three. He and I are working together to try to hold on to this one.

I have ten different apps that I use to keep track of Bob; his travel schedules, his contacts, his expenses, and his families and almost all are open this morning.

He's on a follow up sales call with a Prince so he had to fly commercial to Dubai. He has enough frequent flyer miles to buy out first class but that doesn't immunize him from delays and missed connections. I'm on the line with him trying to find a work around for storms keeping him stranded in Zurich. Definitely, his wife wants him home this weekend, she has missed him so much. She and Bob are both hammer-texting each other with me reading and reply to the texts directed to me by any of them. This is not the first time I've felt like I was standing in a room with them, watching them have a very private argument.

I'm refreshing the Swiss weather site on my main computer screen when Ted Kircher leans in, carrying a heaping plate of my roast beef. He holds it up, gives me thumbs up which indicates that he likes it or that it tastes good, and I smile briefly at him. I set the carved beef out in the conference room with some bread and condiments when I got in this morning and sent a blast email to everyone in I-Sales to come and get it. None of the DALs, like Ted, will touch the bread. Eating out regularly on the road is hell on a diet so all the salesmen still looking for love have sworn off carbs. DAGs will take the bread and make a sandwich with the beef and maybe then add a large slice of the pecan pie. MAHs are rarely in the office.

If they aren't on the road, they are at home squeezing in all the family time they can.

Ted may be hitting on me but it's hard to tell. The salesmen whom are involved in selling multi-million dollar jets are mostly the happy ones. They are always joking, overly upbeat and most times, super friendly. I can take it all as he is coming on to me, but I chose not to. (Refer to rule number one at work.) If I meet them on their level it all stays completely artificial and friendly from a distance. I'm good at walking a fine line between looking accessible and being inaccessible.

Colin, another JetStream sales rep is Geneva working on one of our planes for sales. There is four p.m. train from Zurich to Geneva. I book it for Bob so that he can meet up with Colin there. The storms will have moved east of Switzerland by then and Bob can catch a ride home with Colin and be back in the Savannah by tomorrow morning.

After I have finished the booking, I text him the details:

The limo driver is on the way to the frequent flyer club now. First class train tic in email. Dinner rez on train (carb free). Limo will be waiting in Geneva to get to airport. Colin will hold flight for you. And soothe Kara's ruffled feathers: Bob in Savannah office at 6:48 a.m. Should be home by 8 a.m. Have a great weekend.

Bob replies:

"Perfect as always...thank you from Kara and me."

Kara doesn't reply, but I'm not surprised; she and Bob have been married for almost a year but she is still getting used to the fact that, for better or worse, I'm part of their marriage. If she wants Bob-time she has to go through me because I control his master schedules. I get her as much as I can, but seriously, he has to work too.

As I spin in my chair to take a much-needed pee break I face Cat, another I- Sales secretary. She's holding the tray with what's left of my roast beef and sandwich fixings and the empty pie plate. She drops them in the center of my desk right in front of me.

Your stuff was in the conference room. I need it.

Why does she always make such a big deal out of everything? This girl feeds on drama which I do not have the time or patience for.

Thank you Cat, at least I wouldn't have to go get them later. I smile as I stand and push past her, her cue that this conversation is over. Technically, as the secretary to the senior sales rep I am the senior secretary, but it's not a power I use very often. Being a MAH, Bob is rarely in the office so he doesn't need the facilities here, which means

I don't have to join in the reindeer games of fighting for conference rooms and supplies.

The latest Bob-crisis has kept my mind occupied all morning, but now the remains of my seduction dinner, strewn across my desk, are taking me right back to last night. Before I lose it and go all pity-party at work I gathered them up and head to the kitchen area and the big trash bins. I'll have to throw it all up now. Screw being thrifty and efficient, to hell with saving my plastic serving pieces for another day also. Screw my stupid need to have a plan B and not waste my perfect passion meal—a lot of good all that planning and preparing did me.

I channel my hurt into anger and take it out on the serving platters, slamming them into the wide plastic bin. It fees great and I'm tempted to clean outdated lunches from the fridge for another excuse to throw things. But I stop myself before I act stupid at work, ranting at work is unprofessional and beneath me.

Rounding the corner near the ladies room, I stop dead in my tracks. There's a guy at the end of the hall in a maintenance uniform. The odds of it being Danny are one in a thousand, I know. But my heart thuds anyway as I strain to look for his wide-legged-hands-on-hips Danny-stance. This guy's too tall and lanky.

It can't be him. It's not him. I want to write my racing pulse off to anger, but hell, it looks like my heart and hormones didn't get the memo that my Danny stalking days are over.

Then my traitor brain joins them, seeing the perfect excuse to call Darlene, my dad's old secretary, to find out why one of her maintenance guys is in I- sales this morning. After all, if one of the sales planes is broken I need to know. I mean, this could affect Bob getting home. Of course, she would also know if Danny has switched shifts.

It's one of the new guys. Darlene informs me. —His name's Mark. Why, you likie?

No, I just wondered why he's hanging out in I-Sales.

3-2-B is having landing gear trouble in Morocco and he was the one that worked on it last so they called him in to consult with the repair crew there.

Oh, is the most enthusiastic reply I can muster. If it doesn't affect me or Bob, I let it fall off my radar. I'm also a little occupied trying to figure out clever way to turn the conversation to Danny without being obvious.

Darlene knows me too well, my silence is a giveaway, and she knows it.

He's here, she says, —you want to talk to him or about him?

About him, I answer. I give her the cliff notes version of last night.

He's still on day shift, sweetie, I have no idea why he would tell you that. She says and pauses for my reply but I'm too upset to offer one, and when the silence lingers, she asks, —I've got about five hundred other single guys down here, sweetheart, you sure you don't want one of them? Give me your shopping list, and I'll send one your way.

I chuckle a little at the idea because I know she's only but kidding. Her desk is the social centre of the maintenance hangars. She knows every man and woman who works down there; who's single, who's not and wants to be, and who's about to be.

I want one that's 5'11, medium brown hair with soulful light brown eyes, full lips, great body, can't tell a joke to save his life, polite, punctual, kind.

Darlene lets out a frustrated breath. —Only got one of those and it looks like he's taken by the ghost of wife past, but as far as I know, he still hasn't gone on a date since she left. This is going nowhere so she changes the subject.

How's your dad?

Fine, I say, —He went out with Carla to the casino last week, and he won two grand.

Good for him...Now there's another one who I thought would never date again. I still can't believe your dad left here to get remarried.

I know...I was kind of shocked when he signed up for that dating site, then bam, he meets Carla the first week.

Well, he's one of the few good ones out there. She obviously saw that in him and grabbed him up before it was late.

I sigh, He is, I know, he's just too overprotective and meddlesome when it comes to me.

That's just love, Big Mike style.

I smile and roll my eyes at her too-true statement. My dad is a bit of a legend on the maintenance floor and he was known for helping people out; giving guys their first job out of college or the military, setting them straight when they screwed up at work or at home. He was the mentor of maintenance. He gave Danny his first job when he was fresh out of the Navy and even though my dad is fifteen years older than him they just clicked and became best friends.

Speaking of love, yours just walked by my window with a pissed off scowl on his face. It seems like he always looks that way since your dad left.

I know! I think he's lonely. He needs me Darlene.

Maybe he does, but do you need him? I get the hot part, sweetie, I really get it and don't think I don't stop and take in the view of him working sometimes, but, I mean, don't you want someone closer to your age?

He's only seven and a half years older than me and no, I don't. I feel like I'm babysitting when I date guys my own age.

Yeah, I bet you do, she concedes. —You grew up fast after your mom died.

My phone buzzes and I reach to shut it off so I can continue my conversation with Darlene, but it's Bob.

Bob's calling, whisper, —I need to get this. He's trapped in Switzerland and Kara wants him home now.

And you are the one person who can make that happen.

Or die trying. Thanks for the Danny update. I hang up quickly and take Bob's call, but it's nothing urgent; he's on the train to Geneva and wants to go over next week's meeting schedule so he can stay off his phone once he gets home. Kara's threatened to toss it in their pool more than once. I finish his updates, and then straighten up my desk to make room for my lunch.

I eat alone a lot and often at my desk. Staying several steps ahead of Bob takes extra effort. It took me six years to work my way from being a receptionist to one of the top secretarial positions in the company. I did it by working my ass off, doing extra work, doing more than anyone could or would ask. I've worked with Bob for over a year, and I can say I'm finally getting my strides. I know all his likes and dislikes, I know how to get him in and out of all his most frequent sales stops as quick as possible while maintaining his maximum comfort, I also know his diet, his seat preferences, his shirt size and his favourite tailors.

I sit in my desk and watch the other I-sales secretaries leave together to go out for lunch. I can't say I want to go with them, office gossip wears me out, but maybe I've become too reclusive lately, maybe I'm the one who is lonely and that's why I can't seem to let go of my absurd crush on Danny. I'm resolved to take action now, and I text Dom.

What are we going to be for Halloween this year?

Halloween has always been our thing ever since we were little. We used to coordinate our costumes and trick-or-treat together. We graduated from candy to liquor prizes in high school, but we've always gone out as a team and entered costume contests. I bailed on her the past two years because of work stuff, but I know how to fix that this year. I look up charity Halloween balls in the area while I wait for Dom's reply. Bingo, there is one at the art museum. I copy the link and send it to Kara along with a few very cool, expensive costume ideas for her and Bob. Calendar cleared.

CHAPTER FOUR

I wanted us to go as Wonder Woman and Batgirl but Dom put her foot down because we had done that twice already and she hates her Batgirl costume. She wanted us to make new costumes and go as Green Eggs and Ham but I put my foot down on wearing food costumes which are neither cute nor sexy. Besides any literary reference, even one to a children's book would be lost on the bar crowd. In the end Dom's mama came up with Little Red Riding Hood and the Big Bad Wolf—sexy versions of both, of course. It was a perfect suggestion and solved the solution entirely. I got my cute red dress with a boob-enhancing corset and Dom got to be BAD in her wolf costume.

I take charge of creating our agenda. Since our first Halloween as over twenty-ones, we've had a goal of spending nothing all night. It sort of just happened the first year, but we figured out a system (my analytical issues rearing their ugly head) and have it down to an art now. Step one is carrying no cash on us, just our IDs and cell phones strategically placed in our costumes.

Then we start at the Corner Bar near my apartment, home to lots of skeezy old men and no contest but extremely cheap drinks. It's my dad's old hang out so I rarely have to pay there anyway. Someone who remembers Big Mike will sit and reminisce about him with Dom and me over a couple of three-dollar drinks. Once we have some liquid courage in us, we will have Dom's fiancé, Luis, pedicab us downtown to hit as many costume contests as we can. Even if we don't win the contests, drunk people buy us drinks because they like our outfits. When Luis finishes his pedicab shift at midnight he will bring his car, meet us, and drive our drunk asses home—free and safe.

Dom's mom, Lucca, makes awesome costumes; she's the one who taught me to sew. ..and knit, crochet, macramé, and bake. She's a true Jill of all trades and my organizational idol. She found a tutorial online for making a wolf face with makeup and Dom sits patiently while Lucca and I touch up details and freeze the edges of her long black hair into a frame around her face. She looks evil and hot. Luis should be expecting serious scratches on his back later tonight.

We can walk to the first stop because it's close and, well, we can still walk. The old dudes at the Corner Bar don't disappoint. They buy us cheap shots and throw cliché lines and jokes our way about our costumes. We call for Luis at ten so we can head downtown and catch the first contest at the BarBar. Dom catcalls her fiancé as he peddles.

Hell yeah, babe, look at that ass—dimpled with the promise of pleasure.

Luis is laughing, and I have to admit Dom is right. His job definitely has body benefits, the man has some beautiful legs and a butt I don't mind watching for ten blocks.

BarBar is normally a little too young and goofy for my taste, but I need immature and stupid acts tonight. I love Halloween because being in costume lets me be someone I'm not, someone silly, laid-back, easygoing and fun. Tonight, I'm not Vivienne, the over-organised control freak; I'm Red, the walking trouble.

Dom and I place third in the costume contest behind a girl wearing pasties as a top and some guy dressed as a used tampon (yeah, they keep it classy here). All we win is a bunch of swag from the liquor companies, but it's cool. Some college kids want our prize for their dorm rooms, we trade it for their drinks. While I'm more focused on executing our free-drink, hit every contest plan, Dom is focused on finding a replacement for Danny for me. She keeps pointing out any guy who looks even remotely like he might be my type.

The next bar has the lesser crowd with costumes, and it works to our advantage. We win this one and walk away with $100. Technically this could be drink money but I tell Dom we need to stick to our plan and put this in her wedding fund. I know she's getting pretty tipsy because she hugs and kisses me and keeps telling me what a great fuckin' friend I am.

She doubles up on her search for my next obsession and focuses on a bunch of businessmen who are more than happy to buy us premium drinks on their expense accounts. They're definitely not colleges kids and I don't expect them to look like one. One of them looks particularly good in his suit, but that's just the only spark he got. At Dom's urging, he gives me his card and I see he works for one of JetStream's vendors. I'm glad I'm in costume and for calling myself Red because he is someone I might call for my job.

Dom doesn't hide her compliment, —He was cute! She slurs while we walk to our final contest.

I know but he works for HighTel. I have to call them for Bob sometimes.

So?

So... I don't have an answer because she is starting to make sense. There are no rules against me dating a vendor. I change the subject because I really don't want to go back there. The guy was a good match for me, his only fault is that he isn't Danny and my defences are down enough for me to admit that I still want the lying bastard.

Next stop you have to at least kiss whoever I pick for you, she says defiantly.

I open my mouth to protest, but she shuts it with a glare. She has great taste and knows me well enough that I'm game.

Fine, I'll do it, I accept.

—Hell yes you will. She drags me toward The Rail, our favorite Irish pub, and the place Luis will meet us. As we wait in line to get in, Dom makes some needed adjustments to my costume. I've gone from boobilicious cleavage to my nipples almost popping out and I try to stand still as she adjusts the laces on the front of my corset but the cocktails are kicking in. We get into a giggle fit as the guys behind us encourage her to play with my boobs. I start to play with her hair, stroking it gently and we start moving toward each other like we are about to kiss.

They're chanting, —kiss! Kiss! Kiss!

We're beginning to laugh and none of us sees that the line has moved on.

Move on! The bouncer's yell breaks our little show. I turn to face the bouncer, fishing my ID out of my top and stop.

Danny is sitting on a bar stool in the doorway of The Rail, he was carding people and looking anything but amused. He holds his hand out for my ID. I'm too stunned and dumbfounded on see him, but Dom isn't.

Oh, fuck me!

She gets several offers from the group of guys behind us. Danny gives my ID a cursory glance because he knew how old I am and does the same to Dom's, never saying a word to us. He hands them back and looks past us to the next group in line.

Danny, I. I start to speak, but he ignores me and begins to talk to the guys behind us.

Oh, no way! Dom yells. She has refused to pass through the door now. She's turned Puerto Rican, she-wolf crazy. —Yolo, you think you can treat my girl this way?

She's in his face but Danny just looks up at her slowly and calmly replies,

Please, get inside; I don't have time for this now, Dom.

My heart is pounding loudly now, my head is spinning, and the drinks I have had are threatening to force themselves out on Danny as I push her through the door. On entering, we locate the ladies room and enter there to regroup.

Why would you ever want that asshole? Dom asks angrily. —I don't care what he looks like, he's a fucktard and a loser.

I only half hear her tirade because my fuzzy brain finally pulls the missing pieces together so I can form a thought and sentence.

He didn't lie, I manage to utter.

My utterance stops her cold. —What?

He didn't lie, repeat, this time, saying it to both myself and Dom.

What the fuck are you talking about? She spits out angrily, —so he didn't lie, he just snubbed you, again! She stressed the last word to let it sink deep down in my mind.

No, Dom, he was going to work the other night. He was going to work, here.

I can tell from her look that she is too disgusted with me to grasp the enormousness of what I just figured out. I push myself away from the sink I'd been leaning against and pull on the rickety door handle.

Where do you think you're going? Dom pushes the door shut. There is a loud groan from the girls waiting in line outside the bathroom.

To talk to him. It's obvious that I have to now that I know he's not a liar. I pull on the door again and she holds it closed with her hands.

V, wake up. Whether he lied about the job or not, he just totally snubbed you back there.

No, he's working, he couldn't talk right then.

And you think he wants to talk now?

Damn, she makes more sense drunk than I do. I think for a minute and then say, —Fine... let's just get out of here.

I pull her toward the front of the bar where I can see Danny from where we perch on a window ledge. Dom follows my line of sight and realises that I'm still staring at him.

You're killing me, V, let him go!

No, I say and shake my head, and she settles in. She knows I never give up easily.

UNDYING LUST

CHAPTER FIVE

When Danny takes a break, I approach him, and even though his eyes look like he wants to talk to me, he is however not happy to see me again, and talk with me.

So this is where you work at night? I ask hesitantly.

He just nods, crosses his arms and stands back. He has this fuck-off body language, but I'm not intimidated by it because I know him too well and drunk Vivienne is ten times more tenacious than sober me.

Look, I don't know what I did to piss you off.

He's trying to cut the conversation short and doesn't let me finish.

You didn't do anything, I'm not pissed, I'm just busy, he says and looks away like he has somewhere to go.

I know this isn't a good time or place for this, but I want answers, I want a final declaration of some sort.

My voice sounds whinier than I want it to sound now.

Danny, I just want to know, I mean, you must have figured it out by now.

You need to go home, Vivey, he says, cutting me off and trying to change the topic, —you don't need to be here.

I usually turn to mush when he calls me Vivey, he and my dad are the only two people I ever let call me that. But tonight, it pisses me off because it makes me sound like some child he has to correct and then sends off home to her parents.

What the bloody hell? Why shouldn't I be here? I'm twenty-five years old, its Halloween night and I can be in a bar if I want to.

He finally looks me in the eyes. —It's late. People are getting stupid drunk and I don't want to have to keep an eye on you. I should call a cab for you now.

His last words get me pissed, and I believe my face is as red as my costume now. —I have a ride, and I'll stay as long as I want. You don't need to keep an eye on me—I make the quotation marks with my fingers. —I can take care of myself.

The condescending, patronizing look on his face when he grabs my arm adds fuel to my fire. I twist from his grasp and start to walk away but turn and say, —Screw you, Danny, before I'm too far away for him to hear.

Dom couldn't hear our conversation but she can see I'm livid. She pulls me up to the bar with her and uses her body to wedge us between two guys so we can reach the bar.

I'm sorry, V, I really am, but maybe it's what you needed; It's finally over. She's talking into my ear so I can hear. From her voice, I can tell that she seems happy than sorry.

He treats me like I'm fifteen! I shout at her, angry.

She nods her head, acknowledging that she agrees with me then leans in to talk again. —There's someone here who definitely doesn't think you're fifteen. She turns to look behind the bar and smiles at Sam, my one-night stand.

Hey Sam, Dom hails and waves him over while she is nudges me under the bar.

I'm shocked and dumbfounded to see him. I mean sure, this is where I met him when he was tending bar six months ago, but I hadn't seen him back since or heard from him, not that I was exactly waiting by the phone. Hell, I don't even know his last name. I've always referred to him as Sam the-one-night- stand.

It takes him a minute to recognize Dom and me and I'm a little hurt— yeah, I must have been really memorable. Sam's cute and young, he is a bartender whom I hooked up with some time ago after tons of encouragement from Dom and Irish whiskey. He was my find- another-guy-and-forget-Danny plan then and there's a good chance I'm not the first or last girl to use him for a similar plan.

It's clear when he does place my face and he smiles. I'm relieved, I smile back. —Hi Sam, how's it going with you?

Good, replies beaming at me and I think it's because he's recalling our fling. What can I get you?

Dom practically pushes me out of the way to set up her plan. —V here just got snubbed by this a-hole. So she needs a shot of Jameson

Black Label and maybe some sympathy would go a long way. She winks at him and makes her order, — And I need a shot of Cuervo.

His eyes ask me if it's true; I shrug and nod.

He pointedly says, —Be right back, to me then turns to get our drinks.

Dom leans close to me immediately he's gone to get our drinks. — You have to kiss him.

I have almost forgotten I agreed to let her pick a guy for me to kiss but once again she is right. Round two of the forget-Danny-plans with Sam sounds great right now. Even better, let the asshole see me kiss Sam from his perch at the door—little girl my ass.

When he sets our shots on the bar I let Dom work her magic. She knows that even with a few drinks in me. I'm not forward enough to initiate a lip lock with Sam.

—Too bad there's no one to kiss her and make her feel better, Dom says leaning her head on my shoulder, casting a sad face to Sam.

He laughs at her blatant ploy but reaches his long arm across the bar to the back of my neck and pulls me in for a very nice kiss. I'm flooded with memories of kissing him before and all the other things we did too. As the memories engulf me and the sweetness and softness of his lips sets up a current in me, kiss him back.

The crowd around us gets restless because they want drinks and their bartender is too busy making out with Little Red Riding Hood to make them. Their jeers cause us to pull apart. I want to look over at Danny, but I force myself not to.. I'm dying to know if he saw it and his reaction. Asking Dom is not an option either.

My answer came some minutes later. Dom and I are still at one end of the bar. Luis is there now, too and making out with his very sozzled fiancée. Sam stops by every few minutes to wink at me and occasionally kiss me. It looks like we are both definitely up for round two.

Luis and Dom pull apart long enough to discuss when they are leaving and if I plan on sticking around to wait for Sam to get off work. I spot Sam at the other end of the bar, he is leaning in and listening to someone. When he leans back I see its Danny. Sam looks puzzled, says something to Danny then they both turn to look at me. Holy fuck! He did not just cock-block me. I see myself off my chair, pushing my way toward them.

On getting there, I push Danny aside, it isn't just a push, I rub my ass across his crotch and push him back with my hips. I lean across to Sam and ask him, What did he just say to you?

He looks a little embarrassed when he admits, —He told me you're wasted and I need to leave you alone tonight.

I turn and glare at Danny. He glares back.

What is your problem? I scream in his face. —Who made you my parent?

He's in my face and he doesn't miss a beat. —Your dad did.

You and my dad need to just get the hell out of my life. You both act like I'm a helpless child. I've been taking care of him since I was a kid. I don't need you to babysit me, I don't need your help, and I sure as hell don't need you screwing up my love life!

People around us have begun staring and trying to move away. Danny puts his hands on my hips and tries to steer me out the back door. I hold my stance and push against him. —Back the hell off, Danny! If I want to go home with Sam and screw his brains out, I will and there is no jack shit you can say about it.

There may be no jack shit he can say about it, but there is evidently something he can do about it. He circles my waist with his arm and lifts my feet off the floor and walks toward the back door. We are halfway there, and I'm flailing like a rag doll. My elbow hits the side of his head as I am swinging my hands in protest. I know I'm not very strong, but I'm sure it will hurt.

Vivey, goddammit, stop it! He yells and sets me down right outside the back door. I step back but only to get some momentum to really slam one into his left cheek. He's shocked as I am; I've completely lost control.

I hate myself when I do stuff like this. It's like I hold on so tight to everything in my world then I get some liquor in me and...bam, I do something really stupid without thinking. I try to reach for his cheek but I can't. I think I've broken my hand. I curl up around it, moaning and cussing.

Danny takes a few breaths to calm down and then reaches for my injured hand. I pull it away from him, I don't want him to touch it.

Let me see your hand, Vivey, he says calmly.

I'm embarrassed and still pissed at him. —No, and stop calling me that, stop calling me Vivey!

Tears have welled up in my eyes and I'm almost crying now, fighting to regain some composure but the Jameson swirling through my head isn't helping at all.

I've always called you that, he says, his voice is calmer and softer, his eyes seem to register hurt and he's still reaching for my hand. This is nice Danny. This is the guy who's made me laugh and asked about my life and told me really lame jokes and helped my dad with stuff. This is the guy I put on a pedestal ten years ago; the guy I need to let go of so I can stop hurting myself.

Luis and Dom have come to meet us; they are standing before us now, watching. I look up and see them staring down at me.—Let's go, I say, turn and walk toward the street albeit not knowing or having a clue of where Luis parked his car.

I hear Danny from behind me, calling me, —Vivey.

I don't turn around but I hear the door shut and I assume he's gone back inside. I continue moving.

CHAPTER SIX

It's a rarity for me to travel with Bob, but this week he is speaking at the JetStream Executive conference in Palm Springs, California. It's a strange event where all of us who work together in Savannah get on planes, ours and commercial, and fly to another location to talk to each other.

Bob is delivering a State of Sales address, and then the rest of the time will be spent golfing and socialising with other execs. Kara will be there too doing her exec wife things. I will be stressing out until Bob's presentation is over then he's asked me to come along on a golf outing. I think it's his way of trying to reward me for all my hard work but one, I don't play and two, business social events are almost painfully awkward for me. One on one with someone I know, I'm great but, in a group of people whom I barely know and who outrank me by a mile, I'm tortured.

The best thing about this trip is that I get away from Savannah for a few days and will hopefully be so busy that I have no time to think about Danny and our ugly fight or Sam and the shambles that is my social life. There's no better way to do that than immerse myself in presentation notes.

Dom didn't say much on our way home that Halloween night nor did she say much since after the night. I think she's waiting for my take on the whole debacle. We talk every day, but it's mainly about my trip, her work at the restaurant and her wedding plans, nothing about that night or Danny or Sam.

In retrospect, this whole Danny thing has gotten out of control. He was my first crush indeed so it's only natural that it stays with me for a long time. I was a socially awkward but overly mature fifteen-year- old who was disgusted with boys my own age. Not only was he a smoking hot twenty-three year old man, but he talked to me, like real conversations and paid attention to me. The fact that he was newly married with a baby was incidental. In my teenage brain, I fantasised that he would wake up and realise that his wife was an evil hag and that I was the right girl for him. Then it happened...at least the part where she's out of the picture, although she left him (more evidence that she's completely insane).

So as it happened, I was starting to give up on the whole Danny and me idea until she left. Then it felt too much like fate. Then I waited a year, and another for him to make a move and it's not like he didn't have an excuse to see me. My dad then moved to New Orleans to marry Carla, and this happened the same time as Danny's divorce. Dad asked Danny to keep an eye on me and help me out (which is so annoying in so many ways). This should involve at least him calling or coming by my place anytime to ask how I am, but he didn't.

I've made far too many excuses for him. It hurts like hell to finally face the fact that he isn't interested in me and alone in my hotel room in Palm Springs I have too much time to think. Hell, I could be anywhere and I'd have too much time to overanalyze the why's and why-not's of me and Danny. I 'm actually looking forward to the golf outing as a mental distraction.

It is a beautiful day on the course and the views are stunning. There needs to be a way for introverts like me to get to hang out in beautiful places like this and not have to deal with other people. I'm driving the cart and managing the snacks for the group now, so far, the day has been not too stressful for me. The wives are here so that allows me to fall off the social totem pole and gives me a chance to get to know Kara a little better, although she is mostly busy chatting up the top exec wives. She really is an asset to Bob. I hope she stays.

I've been pretending that I have something engrossing and important on my iPad all day as an excuse not to have to chit-chat. I'm actually reading a BDSM romance book I'm and kind of enjoying it mentally, jumping between the dungeon with Master Raffe and the golf course. I'm on a particular steamy part when I hear someone approach my cart.

Don't tell me you're working out here.

Oh god, it's Joel Rockhurst! Is he really here to talk to me? Why? I ask myself. He's the CEO of the company. He's supposed to stay on the course with his buddies and send some assistant over if he wants a snack. I let out a weak smile.

Oh, no sir, I reply and then I remember what I was actually doing and cover the book and lie, —I was just checking the flights for tomorrow.

He nods his approval and says, —Joel Rockhurst, extending out his hands for a handshake.

Vivienne Ramsey, I blurt out. It's one of those uncomfortable introductions that happen when you know of someone but don't really know them personally. —I'm Bob Brockhaus's secretary.

He nods again then says, —What have you got in there? He glance at the cooler attached to the back of my cart.

I hop out and open the lid. —I have Water, Coke, Diet Coke and Coke Zero.

No tea?

Uhm, no, I reply feeling embarrassed while moving the ice around as if that would make some tea appear. —I could run up to the clubhouse and get some tea for you.

He smiles at me like I gave the answer he was hoping for.

Sweet or unsweet? Lemon? Sugar? Sweetener?

Again I get a approving smile. —Unsweet with extra lemon, no sweetener.

Two lemons?

Two would be perfect.

Be right back, I cheerfully tell as I start the cart and turn toward the club house. I drive fast welcoming the chance to get away from him, he makes me really nervous.

Luckily, once I give him his tea Joel Rockhurst doesn't feel the need to chat with me anymore, but I do catch him looking at me more than once. When I do he doesn't look away like he's been caught. I guess you can look at whoever the hell you want when you run the company. I just can't for the life of me, figure out why.

However, the stare doesn't feel overtly sexual and to top it all up, he's married for the fourth time. The fourth wife is Miss Georgia, they've been married for three years now. She's vivacious, stunning, petite—my complete opposite. I doubt our CEO has suddenly developed a thing for quiet, tall, curvy secretaries.

When we reach the thirteenth hole, I make an excuse about checking on arrangements for tonight's dinner and beg off. Not that I have one thing to do with planning the dinner, but most of them aren't too interested in what I'm up to anyway.

Bob would know I'm lying, but he's engrossed in making sure Kara is having a good time. I'm secretly planning on skipping out on the dinner and taking the rental car to go have dinner alone at In-N-Out Burger, and then find a quiet place near the beach to sit and read my book. It's my true reward for all my hard work.

I convince Bob that I had too much sun out on the golf course and that I'm taking the car to go get aspirin and aloe. It's a semi-valid excuse. I am an Irish shade of pale that is usually only seen on people who are already dead and I've got some red spots on my shoulders where I messed with my mega sun block.

In-N-Out doesn't disappoint, you get what you want and with better pay. We don't have them in Savannah and Bob took me to one when we were in LA and got me hooked. The dinner I skipped was over a hundred dollars a plate (wine not included), but I am so much happier with my cheeseburger, fries and shake. My belly is happy and full and the sun is setting when I find a small public park with benches that have a view of the ocean. I find a bench that is a little out of the way but still looks safe and I get back to my dungeon time with Master Raffe.

I'm more than a little surprised how much this book is turning me on but in real life the idea of being a submissive woman is ridiculous. I've always been smarter and more organised and better at taking care of everyone than anyone else I know, especially men. I would not get frustrated if Master Raffe tied one of the knots wrong then I'd have to show him how to properly tie the ropes (because I would have thoroughly researched and practiced beforehand).

And because I love to shop a lot, I might end up buying everything for our dungeon-time, and eventually I would end up in charge, again. It always happens that way with me, and it can be a great thing, like at work, where I get paid extremely well for it.

Or it can be an annoying thing, like at home, where I did everything and my dad still treated me like I was feeble-minded and couldn't function without him.

I stop overanalysing (at least for a minute) and let myself enjoy being turned on. The heroine is crawling across the floor toward her Master, her leash dragging behind her. She has submitted fully to the god-like figure that is Master Raffe. She is naked (like all his subs) and he is still dressed. She's been good and earned the privilege of time alone with her Master and the opportunity to blow him.

My brain is at war with my hormones as I read this. My brain says she's a simpering moron but my hormones have me thinking I might want to sign up for that opportunity. It's been too long ago I had sex. Sam the-one-night-stand was my last sex six months ago and it was fast, drunk and as clumsy as first time sex always is.

The ringtone I have reserved for Carla pulls me back to reality. I was enjoying my alone time but she rarely calls me so I pick up, she's not one to call just to chat.

Viv? I hear her breath into the speakers of my phone. She's crying and sobbing.

Carla? I ask, but I hear more sobbing. A chill crosses my body and I know something horrible has happened. —Carla, what's wrong?

He's gone, she finally speaks out amidst her sobs. I know who she's referring to, it's definitely my dad.

Gone? As in left you? Did you guys have a fight or something?

No, baby, he's gone. Your dad had a heart attack this afternoon. He died, Viv. He is dead. She starts sobbing again, but this time, it was louder.

There is nothing I can say, I am dumbfounded, I can't seem to find any words. It feels like my throat is closing and I can't breathe. I squeeze on the phone I'm holding to my ear. I'm looking around me, at nothing, trying to grasp something that will tell me this isn't real, that I'm in some horrible dream and that I will wake up in a second.

And just then when I think it's a dream, Carla speaks again. —Oh, my God, Viv! This can't be real. He's too young.

I want to answer her but I still words elude me. The food in my stomach starts to churn, making feel like I'm going to throw up any second.

Viv, are you there?

Yeah, I'm here, I hear myself speak.

Are you at home?

I look around again trying to remember exactly, where I am for everything, seem surreal to me now.

No...I... uhmm...I'm in Palm Springs with Bob, I stutter my response to her. Now my brain has something to grasp onto; planning, organizing. The highly ordered, always-prepared part of me says, — I'm coming there, Carla. I'll get a flight out tonight. I'll be there in the morning.

OK.

I believe you have someone to stay with tonight?

Yeah, I will call my friend Kate.

Good, call her and have her come get you, try to take something so you can sleep. OK?

OK.

Good. Call Kate now, have her stop and get you some sleep meds, then I'll call you when I touch down tomorrow, got it?

Yeah, she answers weakly. I can hear her softening and relaxing a little.

I'm going to hang up now, Carla; call Kate immediately.

I will, she says, and added, —Love you, Viv. It sounds a little odd to my ears, we've never been overly affectionate, but it feels fitting now that she says it.

I love you too, I assure her and I hang up.

I'm in full-on Vivienne mode in seconds, making a mental list of everyone I need to call and all I need to do—book a ticket, talk to Bob, call Dom, call Danny... I'm going to have to put off that emotional punch in the gut for now. Would he even pick up the phone after our ugly fight so I can tell him his best friend has died? I hope he does.

CHAPTER SEVEN

Fifteen hours later, I'm standing at the edge of the security zone watching out for Danny to come through concourse B of the Louis Armstrong International Airport in New Orleans. My flight got in an hour and a half before his so I told him I would rent a car and wait for him to give him a ride to his hotel. He seemed more lost than me when I reached him to break the news.

He must have been at work at the bar judging from the noise level in the background and I was a little surprised he took my call. I played our conversation over and over in my head on the flight, analysing if there would have been a better way or time to call. I also replayed all of my recent conversations with my dad, all of them painfully too short and full of meaningless updates and banter.

I didn't cry at Palm Springs when I told them of the sad news, packed my things and leave. I was too busy hammer-texting with Bob about the hotel and booking myself a flight. Bob offered to try to get one of the company jets for me but I knew that would throw off not only the schedules of the execs but the pilots too. I'm acutely aware of all the work that's involved in getting a private jet from point A to point B, it's not an easy task. It's definitely unlike in the movies where the billionaire makes a call to command an immediate flight somewhere. H o w e v e r , I did accept Bob's upgrade to first class on my commercial flight.

I didn't cry on the flight or after I touched down, although being in the New Orleans airport and realising I'm not going to see my dad hit me hard as I exited the gangway. I felt the pressure, the need to let something out; tears or a primal scream, but this was no place for either. After I claimed the car and got the keys, I lined up with all the happy families and loved ones waiting to greet someone coming home or coming to visit.

While watching a dad lift his son to get a drink from the drinking fountain I realize, I'm an orphan; I have no parents now. So many questions pop up in my mind that I never asked my dad—questions about him, questions about my mom. Questions I would never have an answer to now.

I see Danny approaching, but he doesn't see me, he doesn't seem to see much of anyone. He's just moving forward, he's looking forward but definitely toward nothing. I have to wait until he crosses the security line before I can touch him on the arm to get his attention. He half smiles at me when I do.

Vivey, he says managing a weak smile.

Hey, I half-smile back. There is something grounding about him being here, like part of my dad is here with me now. Despite their age differences they were so much alike. I point toward the parking lot. —I got a car.. .I can go get it while you get your bag and I meet you out front.

This is all I brought, he says holding out the duffle he's carrying.

Oh, OK. Well, then let's get going, I lead the way toward the rental car lot. The ride is uncomfortably silent, the only sound being the voice of the app that's giving me driving directions. When we reach the hotel, I pull up in the drive and while I'm getting a valet ticket, Danny takes all our bags out of the trunk and stacks them so he can carry them all. I have a large suitcase, a hanging bag, a carry on and my briefcase tote because I was planning on being in Palm Springs for a week of semi-formal events. I want to protest, but he lugs them inside without looking back at me.

Bob booked rooms for both Danny and me using his endless hotel points and coveted Black membership status. He sets us both up in concierge level rooms at the JW Marriott downtown. At first, Danny protests and wants to pay but I explain that I'm not paying either and that it's all been paid for by Bob's road warrior life.

I'm going to see Dad and Carla's in about an hour, then Carla and I have an appointment with Dad's lawyer. Do you want to come? I want to establish our schedules before we part ways.

No, his voice is quieter than normal as he replies.

I'll call you when we're done and we can all go to dinner. I want him to come along with us, I want to cling to the part of him that reminds me so much of my dad.

Yeah, sure, he says, drops my bags in one corner of the room and readjusts his duffle on his shoulder as he turns to leave.

I say —thank you but I don't think he hears it over the door closing on its own loudly behind him.

I sit on my bed and I wonder what a normal person would do in this situation. I have always wondered that. Would most people lie down on this giant pillow of a bed and sob? Would they raid the mini bar or call up for a bottle to drown their sorrows? All

I want to do is organize. I don't want the noise of the TV or any distractions as I unpack and make the space my own. I light my soft rose scented candle then arrange my toiletries in the bathroom. I lay out my travel pyjamas and slippers for later. I hang my dresses and contemplate which one I should wear to the funeral and if any need pressing. Oh, screw it. I love ironing. I love rumpled iron clothes and watch them straighten up under the hotness of the pressing iron. I set up the board and press all of them.

I meet Carla an hour later. When I meet her, I see that Carla is my opposite. She isn't wearing make-up and her hair looks slept on. She looks the way someone grieving should look. I look like I'm attending a conference, complete with a notepad in a leather folder for taking notes during the meeting.

She hugs me tight and sobs and doesn't want to let go. It's only when her need for a Kleenex overwhelms her that she pulls away to wipe her nose on a wad she pulls from the front pocket of her jeans. This would be an ideal time to fall apart, to break down while I've got someone here to commiserate with my pain, but I can't seem to get there; I can't cry.

Carla couldn't stop thanking me enormously for being there during the meeting with the lawyer. My dad changed his will when he married Carla and split everything he had between us. I see relief when she hears the news. Before she married my dad she was living on the edge of poverty. She got nothing from her first husband when they divorced and he went to jail. She has three sons for him All of them are grown, but they are more often a financial drain than help to her. I'm not surprised that none of them are here today and I don't expect them at the funeral either.

I really am financially solid without my dad's money and I'm briefly tempted to just give it all to Carla, but I stop myself. If her kids leech off what she gets today, she might need it in the future.

After, the lawyer, we stop by the funeral home Carla, chose to make arrangements. My hackles are up and I'm not sure how to take the amount of upselling we're getting accompanied by a heaping dose of guilt.

I choose my words carefully, —I want this to represent my dad.

Carla nods and splashes her face with water. She starts to take out her cigarettes and then realize she probably can't smoke in here.

Do you think dad would want the premier line casket?

She chuckles, —Hell no, he'd go with a pine box if they'd let us.

I smile at how well she knows him, they've only been married a few years but they were intensely happy, beautiful years for my dad; he and Carla were two peas in a pod.

I'm not trying to be cheap, I assure her. —But I think you will need this money in the future more than we need some of this stuff.

She nods.

So we go with the basic package?

She gives me a firm nod. Like my dad, she's not much of a talker.

I was worried that dinner would be awkwardly quiet and just plain painful with three grieving people. It helped that Carla picked a hole- in-the-wall bar and grill, it's where she and dad liked to hang out. There were the regulars that knew my dad before he died; they were here for the proper Irish wake which involved beer, whiskey and stories all night.

Danny fit right in and had some of the best Big Mike stories since he was friends with him the longest. I shouldn't have been, but I was shocked at some of the scrapes Danny and Dad had with the law. The two of them had worked nights and weekends, fixing up a 1965 Pontiac GTO, or The Goat as they called it. Once it was running, they had to talk their way out of a few speeding tickets when they took it for test spins through the marsh lands outside Savannah. They tried to outrun the cops once, dying to see how fast the car would go. There was no talking their way out of that ticket.

I laugh until I cry at the stories but still can't let go and grieve.

Lack of sleep and too much whiskey overtake me around midnight but none of us is in any shape to drive. I impress the hell out of all the old dudes in the bar when I order an Uber car using my phone and explain how I have an account and don't have to have cash to pay. This brings on rounds of stories of how proud my dad was of me and how he would tell anyone who would listen about his smart, beautiful daughter. I almost lose it then but the car arrives and saves me from becoming a blubbering mess.

In the elevator back at the hotel, Danny watches me. I'm not sure if he thinks I will fall over or burst into tears or if he's analyzing my lack of tears. He looks like he wants to hug me before we part ways at the elevator, but then he grabs my hand and gives it a squeeze.

I wanted a hug, goddamnit, I needed it tonight and honestly, more from him too. I don't know why he barely ever touches me. When I whisper, —Night, Danny, and pull away. I still want so much I can't look at him

SIR PATRICK BIJOU

63

CHAPTER EIGHT

My dad was a man of prestige and great personality. His funeral doesn't do justice to that fact; people don't show up like they are supposed. Although we're not expecting too many people: a few people from the bar, the man dad had been working for and his family and some of Carla's coworkers are the only visitors at the wake. It's strange to be at my own dad's funeral meeting most of the other mourners for the first time. I feel like an outsider and I wonder if it's my own fault. I wanted my independence and pushed him away, and it feels like I'm paying the price now.

Most of the guys he worked with in Savannah, his friends that I know, can't make it on such short notice. They send flowers and make donations in dad's name to his favourite charities and their long-distance love helps me feel a little less disconnected.

Danny stays on the periphery of the event putting on a suit which makes him look incredibly handsome even though he is uncomfortable in it just like my dad. Not being an actual part of the family he has no role, no script to follow like I do to pass these sad hours. I want to go to him, to stand by him and hold his hand but every time I try someone else vies for my attention.

At two p.m. in the afternoon, the funeral director gathers all those present for a brief memorial service. Carla asked me to speak and I struggled with something to say as I lay in bed last night, but the perfect speech eluded me. To do justice to the loving, but frustrating and complicated relationship we had, I would need to speak for hours. Even then I'm not sure I could get it right. When my mom died we became a family of two, but two never felt like a family. It felt more like a couple of people who lived together and crossed paths and sometimes butted heads. We cared for each other and took care of each other, but my mom's absence was like a missing puzzle piece that had tied us together. Big Mike Ramsey, all-American tough guy, did the best he could raising a daughter alone.

I was happy for him when he met Carla and decided to move to New Orleans for her. He had been single for fifteen years (although I learned last night, that he was hardly a celibate). There were days I missed him, but I was mostly happy he had moved on and found love for himself again and most importantly, I was happy to have him out of my hair.

It hurts to even think that now.

But at the time I was ready to make my own life and stop taking care of him and having him jump into my life at the most inopportune times.

There is no way to express how I feel about my dad in a few minutes to a group of people I hardly know so I let the funeral director say a few generic things— a choice I know I will regret later.

Only three people stand in silence as the casket is lowered into the ground. There should be thousands; all the people he had helped and mentored and loved. This is some sick twist of fate that he died suddenly and far from home. To keep myself from facing the stark reality of this moment, I focus instead on all the things I might have done to make this moment better.

I wonder if I had explicitly asked more people to drive to the cemetery for the burial, it would've been better than this. I ponder on if more of his Savannah friends would be here if I had contacted them sooner.

The funeral director is saying a few words now, obviously rounding up his speech. Carla is sobbing, the wad of Kleenex in her hand have reduced to mush. I put an arm around her while I search in my purse for fresh tissue papers to help her with her tears. I can feel Danny's warm presence to my left and for a moment I let myself wish I had someone, specifically him, to hold me up.

I console myself with the truth that I've never had a shoulder to cry on and it would probably feel kind of odd and uncomfortable now. Growing up, it was difficult for my dad to console me when I cried, heck, he never knew what to do whenever I cried. He might pat me on the back and offer a few encouraging words but never a warm embrace. Female tears scared him. I'm better at being the shoulder that others cry on. I may not always know what to say but I'm fantastic at knowing what to do. I focus on Carla, holding her tighter and rubbing her back.

Danny and I pick up some take-out for dinner and take it back to Carla and Dad's place. Although I could use a good dose of cooking therapy right now, but I don't want to invade Carla's kitchen.

Carla's touched that I remember her and dad's favourite Chinese restaurant and her standard order; shrimp lo mien, no mushrooms. It makes me happy because not everyone understands how I love; by paying attention, by remembering their likes and the things that matter to them.

We eat in relative silence and it looks like there might be a long night ahead of us until Carla speaks up.

It's Wednesday night, she clears her throat, striving to sound upbeat, your dad and I always watch Survivor on Wednesdays. Would you want to stay and watch it?

I love the idea of my dad and Carla and all their rituals; the little things that bound them together. Those were the things that made me feel like I was part of a family when I would come to visit them — Sunday afternoon football games, dinner and a movie every Friday night, Wednesdays watching Survivor. Continuing the pattern feels good.

Sounds good, I haven't seen this season.

You two go get it started. I'll bring some dessert; bowls of ice cream eaten in front of the TV were also part of every Wednesday night.

I stand and start to clear plates and close take-out box lids but Carla stops me. —Let me do it, Viv, you've done so much already. Go, get off those heels and get comfortable.

She needs to have a job, a task to keep her in motion and out of her head so I go to the bathroom to gather myself and make sure I don't have mascara pools under my eyes.

When I walk into the living room Danny is sitting where I normally sit on the couch, he has unbuttoned his shirt about half way down to compensate for the house that is not air conditioned. It's embarrassing how much it affects me, even today. My lust for him has no bounds, no conscience, and obviously no scruples.

I figure I had better play it safe and not sit on the couch with him. Carla 's chair and dad's recliner surround a small end table on the other side of the room. I decide to take dad's lumpy, old recliner but I stop before I can cross the room, my heart is lurching. I feel like I've been sucker-punched in the gut, the stupid chair is my undoing.

My dad and I had had a steaming argument when I was sixteen and I was going through an HGTV/DIY phase of redecorating. I had a plan for our living room and I wanted my dad's fugly recliner gone. There was no place for it in my design plan. As I look at it now, I hear all the ugly things I said to him about cheap-ass furniture and him being stubborn and unreasonable. I called him an asshole that night, I think aloud, remembering that day.

I'm stuck, I can't move. I'm silently crying and sobbing when I hear Danny call my name.

Vivey? I don't answer because I can't seem to get out of this sad place. I'm in deep, trying to wish my dad back so I can apologise. I wish I had more time with him.

Danny appears next to me and I hear him quietly say in whispers, —Vivey.

The ball of emotion that had been caught in my chest since Palm Springs rises and I can't stop it. I double over and gasp for breath as Danny begins to rub my back, unsure what to do for me. I collapse on to him as my need for comfort overwhelms me. He pulls me down with him onto the couch and holds me close while I sob.

Tears and snot are pouring out of me and the harder I cry, the closer he holds me until it's almost hard to breathe with his strong arms compressing me; I'm falling apart and he is trying to hold me together.

He's gone, I choke out then hiccup as I try to breathe in.

Danny smooths my hair with one hand while the other keeps me pinned to his shoulder. I feel him breathing unevenly, fighting his own pain and tension.

I want him back, I wail.

I know. His voice cracks and I realise that he is crying too.

I fling my arm over his other shoulder and turn my face into his neck and hold him tight. Danny smells of cologne mixed with the underlying scent of jet fuel, the scent that always clung to my dad's skin too.

When I finally calm myself enough to stop crying I'm spent. I don't know when I've ever felt this exhausted. I struggle to lift my head from Danny's shoulder, but he pushes me back down and gently kisses me on the forehead. I muster enough strength and squeeze his shoulder while I leaning onto him and kiss his neck. It feels so natural, kissing him, probably because I've conjured it up so many times in my mind. I kiss him again and this time, I feel a rush of endorphins wash through my tired brain. I turn my head to kiss his jaw. His whiskers feel exactly like I knew they would against my lips; sensual and rough.

I must have shocked him because he turns his head toward me and there they are, the most kissable lips I've ever seen and loved. It's more instinctual than planned when I lean up and gently kiss them. They feel just as good as I knew they would. I kiss him again, and I get blindsided by a wave of lust. I want more. I want to kiss his warm lips for hours.

I want to feel them all over my body, everywhere I hurt, kissing away all my pain and tiredness.

Just as a little voice starts to remind me that Danny doesn't want this, that he doesn't want me, he kisses me back and I shove that little voice away and let myself fall into this wonderful floating feeling. I feel almost drunk, definitely out of my head, for once. I'm only vaguely aware of Carla coming into the room, we pull apart, but she has seen us already.

She chuckles and shakes her head, —He always wondered when you two would get together.

Her words stun both of us and we turn and look at her in unison.

He would talk to you on the phone, she gestures to Danny with the bowl of ice cream she's carrying, — then after he'd hung up, he would always say that one of these days you were going to pull your head out of your ass and finally grab onto Vivey.

Danny is too stunned to speak. All I can do is laugh at the irony and the way Carla quoted my dad perfectly.

He turns to me and asks, —Did you?

Know? I shake my head, —No, he never said anything to me. But it would have been nice. There is too much-left unsaid.

Carla hands us each a bowl of ice cream smiling like a Cheshire cat. She unpauses Survivor, then sits down with her own bowl.

I eat my ice cream and try to focus on the show but I can't stop looking back at Danny. He looks like he is going over every conversation he ever had with my dad about me. He's so lost in his thoughts that his ice cream melts before he ever takes a bite.

CHAPTER NINE

We finish watching Survivor with Carla and then linger on our goodbyes, promising that we will come by tomorrow before we fly home. I know she's spent nights here without my Dad before but it's still hard to leave her alone tonight.

Danny is still quiet on the car ride to the hotel. I catch him stealing glances at me occasionally.

What?

He shrugs.

Talk to me, I say and search for his hands, to grab and hold them calm me, but I can't seem to find where his hand is right now.

Do you remember when you moved into your apartment?

Yes, I do remember that day vividly. That night, my dad, Dom and Luis were all around to help me move in my things, but Danny remained back when others had gone just to help me set the bed right. It was rather coincidental that everyone else aside Danny had somewhere to go that night. It was yet another time that I pretty much threw myself at him and he told me no.

Yeah, I remember, I finally answer him.

He's watching the road but lost in thought, —I wanted to stay.

Now it's my turn to be shocked, I try to speak but don't know where to start from or what to even say. He doesn't notice this because he's still lost in thoughts albeit his eyes focused on the road and his driving.

It was about two months after she left.

I know he means his wife, he never says her name.

I told myself that I was rebounding, that your Dad would kill me, that you'd regret it. But I wanted to stay.

But you never...I didn't think you liked me. I mean, I thought you were only nice to me because of my Dad.

He seems to be clouded in a train of thoughts which makes him not to reply to what I said immediately, or like he is thinking of the right words to use to pass his message to me.

I've made attempts to drive by your place often. He says chuckling and turns to me, —I've thought about just stopping by, pretending to be checking up on you, just to hang out with you for a while.

Why didn't you?

He shrugs and turns his face back to the road but then replying, —It wouldn't have been a good idea, even if I didn't think Mike would kill me, I was usually feeling sorry for myself.

But I would have...

Not fair to you, And there it is again him and my Dad, thinking for me, telling me what I want and need, never asking my opinion.

Don't you think that's for me to decide? I know how to take care of myself, Danny.

He stresses his sincerity by looking over at me, —I know you do.

He remains quiet and the rest drive to the hotel is driven is silence. When we get to the hotel, he touches me more than he has ever touched me since I've known him. He offers his hand to help me out of the car then holds mine in the elevator. He must be still torn about us because his head is bent low, probably studying the floor or lost in thoughts. He finally looks at me when we hear the chime that we've reached our floor.

When the door opens, he lets go of my hand and steps off. I follow and stand there waiting to see if he'll tell me what he's thinking now.

I'm not going to tell you what to do, he says to me while I feign shock on hearing that, —But I'm going to lay it all out here.

He takes my hand and studies our entwined fingers, —I'm too old for you, I'm broke and I have a bitch of an ex-wife.

I knew all these things so he doesn't waste time getting into details. He brushes through them and then he studies my reaction when he says, —And I'm leaving.

My heart jolts at the last word, —You're leaving? What do you mean you're leaving? Where are you going?

I've taken a job in Saudi Arabia, he replies me, —I leave in two months time.

He squeezes my hand while I remain mute and shocked.

This is a bad time to tell you about this, Vivey, I'm sorry. I want you to know before we.

Why? I interrupted him even though I already know why. There's always a need for aeroplane mechanics in Saudi and it pays a shit ton, tax free. Guys go there to make real and cool money.

Remember when Nick was born, he had that heart thing?

I nod. Danny's son was born not long after I met him. He was premature and had a heart defect but I thought all that was taken care of. He had several surgeries when he was little to fix it.

Well, there's been complications. He's doing OK now, but he's on some new experimental drug and treatment and it's not covered by insurance.

Oh, I nod. That explains a lot about him being broke in spite of his two jobs.

I've signed a three year contract there, he says.

I nod again and exhale my frustration. It feels like a sad joke; after ten years I find out that he wants me and he's leaving. We've both know that we're completely emotionally wrung right from the funeral and now this.

He leans in and rests his forehead against mine and says, —I'm sorry. He puts his other hand on my neck and pulls me in for a hug, oblige. I say I'm sorry too into his collar.

What are you sorry for?

For me, for you, for us, I sigh and burrow farther into his warm neck. —For Carla, for my Dad.

My voice cracks and he holds me closer with both arms.

Come sleep with me. I feel him start to pull away then I add, —I mean sleep, as in go to sleep. Don't let me lie there alone in my room and overthink all of this.

How can I stop that?

By sleeping next to me, definitely without this annoying shirt you are putting on, I bump his collar with my nose, —I won't be thinking about much of anything else when you lie next to me.

He laughs softly and kisses my forehead, —Alright, we'll just sleep and nothing else.

I can tell he's as tired as I am but there's still a question in his voice that that's all we'll do.

In my room, we strip together; I watch him take off his socks and shoes, jacket and shirt but leaves his suit pants on. I unbuckle my shoes and toss them on the floor then pull my dress over my head. I stop momentarily trying to remember which bra and undies I have on. I look down, it's my pink lace set. It's more sweet than sexy but it makes me feel pretty when I'm sad. Danny raises his eyebrows at it and smiles; I pull back the covers and slide into bed while he remains standing there as I slide into the bed.

—That's what you're wearing to sleep?

I nod in response and pulled back the covers on his side to join in. He shakes his head in protest, but then he slides in between the sheets and turns off the lamp before settling himself on the pillow. I scoot across until my head is on his chest and my leg wrapped around his.

I'm supposed to sleep like this he asks caressing my back.

For now, I breathe out relaxing on his chest.

You're not making this easy, he complains.

I don't want to, is my drowsy reply before I drift off saving him from more of the torture.

I don't care if it's only for a short time but I'm awake and have been awake for almost a half an hour, just lying here watching Danny sleep and trying not to move and wake him. When he told me he was leaving last night, I was crushed, so crushed I had to push it aside and forget about it so I could get some sleep. When I woke up this morning I knew exactly what I want to do, I want to be with Danny for as long as I can.

I've been thinking about my Dad and Carla, would they have missed the chance to be so in love, if they had known it would end so soon?

Hell no! I'm glad my Dad Quit his job to move to New Orleans and be with Carla. I'm glad that he had those few years when he wasn't lonely anymore, his life is giving me my answer.

I reach for Danny's hand and lace my fingers with his.

I touch my cheek to his warm skin and breathe in, I'm imprinting his smell on my brain, it makes me so damn happy. He twitches and mumbles then rolls onto his back and slowly opens his eyes. I smile and look up at him with my chin on his chest.

Good morning.

He doesn't respond to my greeting, think maybe he isn't a morning person, but he surprises me by moving his arm from under me to around my shoulder and pulls me in close. We lie there in companionable silence for a long time.

I thought about what you said last night, and I don't care if it's only for a short time.

With my head against his shoulder, I can't see his face, but I can hear him take a deep breath as he thinks about my answer.

Do you think my Dad would have stayed away from Carla if he had known it would only be for a few years?

He rubs my arm for a few minutes before he says, — No.

His stares are at the ceiling; he's probably deep in thoughts.

I get why you're leaving, though I don't like that you are, but I get it.

I take my hand from his and rub it up his arm. He has a faded farmer's tan on his bicep where his uniform shirt ends. I've noticed it before and wanted to touch him there. I do.

Let's just do this, for right now, for the time we've got.

I caress his forearm, the muscles and tendons I've watched bunch and flex while he worked with my dad. I want to touch him everywhere and get him turned on (I'm really getting turned on), but I'm not feeling much movement from him. I pull away to see his face.

He's contemplating on it again.

What? I ask him.

He shakes his head and laughs, —I should warn you, it's been almost two years, Vivey, two fucking years. He looks down at me, —I don't want this to be bad but...

I don't understand. I would think after two years of no sex he would be on me like white on rice. I want to roll on top of him and get this party started with already, so I start to and he eases me off.

Vivey, do you know what happens when a man hasn't had sex in two years?

I have to admit I don't. I shake my head without saying a word.

I'm gonna feel like when I was a teenager, Vivey and this maybe really quick. You are fucking killing me right now, babe.

I had noticed the tent in the sheet but figured it was just morning wood. He might have been trying to warn me off by telling me that he was going to be bad in bed, but all I heard was that I was killing him. I feel like a goddess that can turn this handsome man on.

I know my smile is wicked but I can't help it, I'm having too much fun. Drive you crazy and kill you with sex? Challenge fucking accepted! I lean down and kiss his chest, then his sternum, his belly button and the start of his happy trail.

Goddamn, Vivey! I can hear his conflict, Stop, but...don't.

I sit up and unbutton his pants then unzip it slowly. I reach in and scratch my nails along the fabric of his boxers, against the length of him.

He grabs onto the pillow behind him with both hands, he is feeling the pleasure mounting up. Yeah, you'd better hold on.

I pull his pants and his boxers with my hands and toss them aside, on the floor.

Oh, hell yeah.

He has those indents on the hip which point to my prize. I want to taste him and know how he tastes like, but I restrain myself a little and use my hand to caress him. He's rigid and pulled up tight and I realize that he won't last long so I dive in. I take as much of him as I can in my mouth then try to relax and take in more, past my gag reflex. I hear a sharp inhale followed by a raspy exhale. His reactions are making me feel even more powerful.

I work him with my tongue, he lets out curse words interspersed with my name. It spurs me on to work him even harder and more sensually. He reaches for my head when he's about to come and holds on to me. I don't know if he wants me in a certain place or is afraid I'll let go and stop but I won't until he's spent and uttered the name of every deity he knows and added mine to the list.

I fall back onto the bed and laugh, conceited with my prowess. I fucking rocked his world.

And that is just the beginning; round one.

CHAPTER TEN

It seems I was a little premature, feeling smug and thinking I had a few things to show Danny. Round one took the edge off of him, the two year build-up of sexual tension. And it made round two an eye-opening lesson for me on the difference between sex with a man and sex with boys.

I thought I'd had pretty good sex in the past, I mean it was fun and felt good. But it was all like quickie or half-baked sex; rushed and quick, serves a purpose, just the basics. I thought that was all there was until Danny introduced me to gourmet sex and boy was I satisfied?

Sure, I had always assumed he 'd be good in bed because one, who fantasizes about crappy sex and two, there's something in his walk, an ease in his own body that just said that he would be uninhibited and confident, I got that part right. But I didn't know that was just the tip of the iceberg, the part of this incredibly sexy man that the world could see. What I got this morning is a fantastic lover; something I thought only existed in steamy romance novels.

The first idea he erases is that sex is just the actual act, tab A in slot B. After his mind-blowing blow job, he's in no hurry to go again whereas I'm definitely ready. I try to move things along, reaching for him, wanting to get him hard again. But he takes my hand off and laces it with both my hands over my head and rolls half onto me. I'm trapped, in the best way, at his mercy for him to set the pace.

Leaning into me, he nudges the tender skin on my neck with his lips and stubble setting off a ripple of sensation through my body.

Slow down, he whispers to my ears.

I hate it when someone tells me what to do, so with that in mind, my knee-jerk reaction is to do the opposite. But then I realize that he's right. I've wanted this (what's happening this very minute) for years. I've dreamed about it and now that I'm here I'm going to rush through it? I don't think so.

I stop fighting him, pushing against him, and relax under his weight. It feels so good.

That's it. He's trying to encourage me but all I hear is patronizing. I'm having a hard time letting go of the fight that we've been having for the past two years and I tense up again, he notices.

What's wrong?

What's wrong? What's wrong is that I'm me—uptight, neurotic, overbearing me.

Vivey, relax.

Nerves and frustration bubble up into a laugh. —Me, relax? When have you ever seen me relaxed?

He knows me well enough, and that reply from me made him chuckle. —I haven't, but I want to, I want to see you relaxed.

He leans in again and slowly presses his entire body to mine and gently slides up and then down.

I want to make you feel good but I can't if you won't relax.

He's ignited nerves all the way to my toes; every inch of my body wants him, he's exciting parts of me that I'd never thought about during sex. The front of my thighs can feel the hair on his legs and the muscle beneath and they want more. My belly feels soft against his while my breasts are tickled by the hair on his chest. He's moved from kissing my neck to my shoulders then my clavicle. I doubt most other guy would know where my clavicle is let alone how kissing me there would fire so many sensitive nerves.

I can feel him starting to get hard again but he's still in no hurry, he's meticulously making his way down my body, blissfully torturing me. My urge to take over and get relief is overwhelming even when I try to subdue it.

I try rubbing my hip against him but he pulls away, denying me access. I scoot closer, he sets his strong leg over my hips and keeps me in place. What the hell is wrong with me? I'm turning lovemaking with the man of my dreams into a wresting match.

I can't hide my tension, he stops kissing me and let's go of my hands. I'm sorry.

He rolls me onto my side and spoons me from behind. It's alright, first times together are never easy. We lay there for a minute making love and I worry that he's giving up on me.

Please don't stop, I say and immediately regret it. I can't believe that I'm begging now. Please have sex with the insane control freak.

I can feel his lips smile against my shoulder. I haven't, I'm still holding you down.

He pulls away from me and I panic, maybe I've pushed him too far.

Stay right there, he says and gets out of bed. I'm so relieved he'll be back that I ignore the fact that he just gave me a command. I roll over to my side and lay supine watching him from the bed.

He finds his wallet and digs deep into the lining before producing a smashed, battered condom pack. Flipping it around in his hands, he asks. Do these expire?

I laugh and relax and fall more in love with him—the wonderful laid- back man who can stand there naked and make jokes. I hop out of bed and dash into the bathroom for my toiletries bag and my own supply of condoms. I whip out five fresh condoms and toss them on the bed. Danny's eyes trail to the bed and see the condoms, he raises an eyebrow at me. I'm not sure if he's impressed that I'm prepared or worried that I carry condoms with me.

What? he exclaims softly and picks them, - five?

I laugh, —I could get more if we need them.

He opens one and slides it on as I watch. His openness with his body makes me less concerned about mine. I take off my bra and toss it across the room then my panties which I slingshot in his direction, I miss by a mile, but I don't bother. I'm just having so much fun.

He sits on the bed with his back against the headboard and motions for me to join him with what a tone that sounded like a command.

Come here.

I fight the momentary urge to go against his directive and climb onto the bed next to him. He uses my hips to have me straddle his lap, his cock so close to where I want it.

We'll do this your way, this time, he says and pulls me in for a kiss and lets me push my hips into his, grinding against him. But you will let me have my way with you eventually.

With that he slides his hands down to my ass and lifts me onto him. I sink down then kneel up again, revelling in the sensation. —That's it, you've got control, now make yourself feel good.

His permission is like a gift, more like an acknowledgement that he understands me, it opens me up and releases my fears of failing him. I lean in and kiss him, trying to let him feel how much he means to me. His moan of pleasure is music to my soul because I'm pleasing him. I'm in control and he's, not just tolerating it, he loves it.

I get out of my head, and just feel and our sex moves into an entirely new realm—a dance of give and take. I don't rush, pushing for my orgasm. I know it will come and I can feel it building. I slowly ride him and when he bends his knees, I fall back onto them, enjoying the different sensation of the new angle.

He uses my hips to help me when I speed up the rhythm of the ride. I'm so close when I feel him piston his hips and he comes with a loud moan of my name, mixed with random religious sayings and cuss words. As he comes, I feel my orgasm coming, it feels like never before because I'm not lost in my own head, worried about my performance, I can feel him pulsing in me. Oh my god, it's such a turn on, I'm so close to coming. I reach down between us and use my fingers to push myself over the edge, almost screaming his name with each wave of a spasmodic jerk in response to the orgasm I'm having.

I fall back after I have come; a euphoric, spent pile of mush and I laugh at nothing because I don't do it often enough. We lay there catching our breaths and Danny smiles at the ecstatic feeling of sex he has had with me. I don't know what to say. What I feel is beyond words. Luckily he doesn't seem to be looking for conversation either.

He pulls me forward, against his chest and slowly eases himself out of me as we stretch out on the bed.

When I finally get the energy to speak, all I can say is, —Wow.

He lazily rubs his hand along my arm. —Wow?

He's questioning this? Did he not just have mind-blowing sex with me? Or is he questioning whether he was that good?

It dawns on me then that, despite his substantial skills he hasn't used them on a woman in a long time, let alone an appreciative woman. Could his crazy-bitch of an ex really have not appreciated sex like that? Or would they even have been having sex in the end?

I never knew what really caused their splitting, I never asked, and the only little I knew is gotten from bits and pieces I overheard. But one thing I do know is that she left him for a guy with more money—a lot more money. She's a member of the elite of Charlotte now, something Danny could never give her.

Leaning up to his chest, kiss him and say, —Yeah, wow.

CHAPTER ELEVEN

The next morning, we are at Carla's house and the realisation that we'll be finally leaving her completely alone make us delay our inevitable leaving. She digs through drawers and papers, offering me stuff I might want or need. On Dad's dresser top she finds pictures of me as a kid and a few of my dad and mom's pictures together; I put those in my purse.

What about The Goat? She asks when she comes across the keys to the car Danny and my dad had fixed up.

I answer her but look at Danny. —What about The Goat? It's more his than mine.

It's yours, she says and hands me the keys. —I've got the Ford and I can't drive that thing.

Danny eyes are on the keys, I can see that he wants it. He did half the work on it and it's his tie to my dad.

With the keys in my hand, I hold them out to him motioning him to take them, but he shakes his head, —It's yours, he left it for you.

But…

But you do know I can't take it with me anyway, he cuts me short, and just then I remember his new work he got at Saudi.

Carla sees another opportunity to keep us with her for a little while longer.

Well, let's go see if the darn thing even starts. It's been months since he drove it.

I hand Danny the keys. It can be finicky when you started it and he would know how to finesse and coax it. I actually know how, but this isn't the moment to let him know that Dom and I had borrowed the car a few times through the years.

The moment it turns over and roars to life, we are all still and silent. The ambience of the garage now feels like my dad is here; the loud sound, the oversized energy, the precision of the mechanics is all Big Mike's signature in this world. At that moment, I want the car and I want Danny to have it too; we both need this piece of my dad.

We drive around a few blocks, letting the battery charge, all of us silently enjoying the feeling of my dad's presence and when we finally get back to the house, none of us wants to get out of the car.

I sit there in the driveway and think for a spell on what to do and when I'm done thinking, I let them know what I finally concluded within me.—I guess I'm driving this home.

Today? Carla asks.

Yeah, I say and nod my head, picturing the perfection of the idea. Then my perfect idea grows, fate giving me a nod that Danny and I

should have more time together.

You coming with me? I ask Danny.

He doesn't answer right away, but I know he can't resist me driving him and Dad's baby back to Savannah. He looks around the interior assessing the odds off the car making it six hundred and fifty miles.

Yeah, I can't let you drive this thing home alone, I'm not sure it'll make it, he accepts the invitation which makes it sound like he's back to treating me like a child again.

I smirk at him, and what are you going to do if it doesn't?

He smirks back, I'm the mechanic that built it. I'm sure I can think of something. What do you think you would do alone?

I lift up my phone and pointed to the AAA app. They have tools, you don't.

Carla laughs at us from the back seat, I wish I could be there to see the two of you on this road trip.

I smile back at her and point to my texting app. —I'll send you updates.

I return the rental car back to the rental company, cancel our flights and stop at a huge truck shop on the edge of the city to shop for some provisions. It's few minutes to seven p.m. in the evening, and the sun is setting in the horizon now.

Why don't I drive to Mobile while you sleep then we can decide whether to take I-10 through Florida or go through Alabama, I suggest while we walk Danny though the store, gathering snacks.

One, you aren't driving, I am, and two, we are not going through Florida, he says and pours himself a large cup of black coffee after we are done gathering the snacks we will need.

I hand him two sugar packets which seems to startle him, Two?

It's a large cup, I note, pointing at the 32 ounce coffee cup. He doesn't reply, he collects the sugar packets empties them both into his cup.

My app is showing six construction zones on the Alabama route, I notify him. It might be forty miles longer though Florida, but it will be much faster and easier to drive.

He takes the phone from me and silently studies the map on my phone. Fine, he says, Florida, whatever.

And you are not going to drive the entire way; throughout the journey.

Vivey, you can't handle that car. It's fast; the steering has too much give---

And the brake pedal sticks, I finish for him. I've driven it, many times, I finish and let him process that bombshell while I peruse the selection of granola bars.

Big Mike let you drive that car?

Dom and I borrowed it a couple of times, and I'm pretty sure my dad didn't know about it. I grab two protein bars to go with my iced tea.

You stole the car.

They he says it, it sounds irritating to me. We've started something new but it's not going to be easy to let go of what we've been to each other this past few years.

I don't reply to his accusation because I want to tell him where to stick it and not in a sexy way. Instead I walk toward the register and ask if he wants an apple or banana from the fruit basket as we pass it.

He refuses to sleep as I had suggested. But he decides to test my driving skills with the car by letting me drive the first leg of the trip to the Mobile. I keep it just above the speed limit and obey all the traffic laws even though I'm itching to push it. Driving it pumps back great memories of cruising it down long, roads with the windows wound down and the stereo turned up. I laugh to myself at the memory of Dom throwing herself at the cop who stopped us. At eighteen, she was more silly than sexy and in the end, I'm pretty sure the cop let us go because he was impressed with the car, not us.

When I let him take over on the far side of Mobile, he visibly relaxes, like he'd held his breath the entire time I drove. He eases back into the seat, lets his hand drape across the steering wheel and gear shift, and tunes into the powerful hum of the engine. God, he's so sexy even at that. And then there's the good old front bench seat, just calling me to unhook my seat belt and stretch across it to christen my new car with a little highway head. I decide that now might not be the time but only because we have hours of driving ahead of us. He might be more receptive to killing time that way later.

The sun has set and the early fall night air is cool in the quiet, sparsely populated Florida panhandle. I don't sleep because I want to talk to him; I want to try to find the kind, attentive man who I fell in love with, the one who existed before my dad left and assigned him the job of my keeper, the one who had an open heart before his wife left him.

Our conversation during the trips flows like magic, and we keep talking to each other, while he drives. We start to fall back into the friendship we had when I was younger. We talk about many things, and we digress to his son's health, he opens up tells me his heart relapse, the experimental drugs he's taking, and the costs.

One shot, just one damn shot, was over two grand. And he had to get the shot for six months in a row. He shakes his head in frustration. —That put me behind, and then he had a reaction to the shots and was in the hospital for a few weeks—scared the shit out of me. That was partially covered, but I sold my car to make all the deductibles on that.

I seat and allow him to vent all about it, offering some comfort because I don't think there's been anyone he has discussed it with. But, while he vents on, find it difficult to listen to him. (I've been programmed to fix and not listen). If someone presents me with a problem I can't help but find a solution. And like the pieces of a puzzle falling into place, I see it. I know how I can help Danny get back on his feet faster and give us some time together. The problem is that the guy who sees himself as taking care of me will probably be less than amiable to moving in with me.

CHAPTER TWELVE

Hell no!

Yeah, I know that's pretty much what I figured he would say. He's insulted so I just need to lay out all the reasons why my idea is flawless.

If you move out of your house now it will be easier to sell and then that will be taken care of before you leave. I can help you get rid of stuff and put things in storage. In fact, I'm gonna need a storage garage for this car. We can get a bigger and better and we have it split so that can store your stuff in there while you're gone.

He doesn't respond right away so at least he's mulling it over. He takes so long to reply and just when I think he's not going to he finally says, —I can't mooch off of you. I should be thrilled because it sounds like he might be willing, but his harsh view of himself and the situation stops me short.

Danny it's not... I start to give him my logical perspective, that we're friends helping each other out but I realise that there is no room for reason here. It's killing me to see him hurting so much and to know I have a solution. If he would just see it from my point of view.

I drop it but it still sits heavy between us. I wish I hadn't said it. I didn't mean to kick this good man when he was already down. We drive for long in silence after that little misunderstanding, we have nothing to say to each other for the next few hours.

The sun is coming up and Danny looks exhausted, so I check the hotel app on my phone.

There's Fairfield coming up in Jacksonville. They have free breakfast so we could eat and sleep for a few hours.

I'm trying to be helpful but it seems to irritate him more. —I'm not going to let you pay for a hotel room, I'll get some coffee and we'll keep going.

I would let him be right for once if his plan wasn't so dangerous. He needs sleep if he's going to keep driving and it doesn't look like his crushed male ego was going to let me take over anytime soon.

I'm not paying for it, I say quietly, —Points, I remind him.

Bob's points?

Technically, yes, but they're also my points to use, you know, he never uses them and when he's not traveling for work, he doesn't like to go anywhere. He briefly considers it then shakes his head in the negative. I change tactics.

Danny, I'm tired and hungry, I'd like to take a shower and change clothes. I hate resorting to a take-care-of-me plea but we need to stop and it's a way that puts him back in charge, but I don't mind, I add, please.

Fine, tell me where to go, he says with a resigned breath.

We pull over in the next hotel and enter to have breakfast. The breakfast is served, and we eat in silence with our focus on the news being reported via television at the far corner of the room; our silence is a painful reminder of how much I've already screwed things up.

In our room, I shower first and when I finish I announce that its his turn but he's sound asleep on one of the two double beds. I stand there and watch him, he is wearing only his briefs; his large, beautiful male body sprawled across the bed. I begin to get chilled, my hair is still wet and I'm wearing only a towel in the air conditioned room.

I want him; I want his warmth, I want his affection; his arms around me, his heart beating close to my ear. I think about taking the other bed and leaving him alone but then I remember my Dad and Carla and their short time together. Carpe diem, girl. I peel off the towel, lay it on the pillow and slide into the small space available next to him.

He wakes briefly and looks at me, I look back, pleading with my eyes, completely vulnerable, raw and naked—risking a very painful rejection. He gives in but huffs out a frustrated sigh before he pulls me in close to him and spoons around me. This is, not the way I had pictured things between us, not what I had hoped for.

I wake up in the afternoon with the afternoon sun seeping in through the cracks in the drapes. I'm facing Danny's chest while breaths deeply and I watch, mesmerized by the rise and fall of his chest. I reached out to caress him and tentatively touched one of his nipples, wondering if that would feel as good to him as it does to me. He rolls on the and smiles in his sleep, interesting.

I take one of his nipples in my mouth licking it and then scrape it a little with my teeth. He moves closer to me, instinctively pushing his sleep-erection against me. I slide one leg over his hip and revel in the sensation.

He's still half asleep but I'm entirely turned on and desperately wanting that sexual high and connection with him again. I reach down and stroke him through his briefs, and then reach inside the waistband, wanting to feel more.

That gets his attention, he opens his eyes and smiles lazily at me.

I could get used to being woken up this way, he says to me in whispers.

I like the way he says it, it's like he's warming up to the idea of us living together.

I could get used to waking you up this way, I smile back and slowly stroke him, trying to replicate the speed he likes. It feels so good; physically, sure, but more than that. At this moment I feel close to him, connected, like we're a couple.

CHAPTER THIRTEEN

We drive up after the sex at the hotel, we reach the outskirts of Savannah when the sun is setting and I'm plotting the logistics of Danny and me staying together tonight. Unfortunately, I don't see any way for it to happen, especially when we both have to go to work tomorrow. I reluctantly ask him to drop me at my place so he can take the car to his house.

We get to my house and pull over in the parking space. We unload my things, blocking all the parking spaces behind my building. I take my carry-on bag and Danny grabs the rest. As we are coming up the back steps, my neighbour, Mrs Ogden, opens her door.

Vivienne, she calls out, I thought that was you.

She looks at me briefly then studies Danny and says to me, —I haven't seen you around much lately.

Yeah, I've been out of town, I just got in now, were you looking for me? I enquire.

Oh no, I'm fine, but I took a delivery for you and I haven't seen you around to give it to you. She seems a little irritated, which is odd, I mean, we accept packages for each other all the time.

Oh, OK, well I can take it now.

She slips inside her door and returns hidden behind the largest bouquet of flowers I have ever seen outside of a hotel lobby, I have to step back to make room for the oversized arrangement between us.

Wow, thank you for taking them, Mrs. Ogden, I really appreciate it.

There's a card, but it's sealed. I can see her watching Danny for a reaction out of the corner of her eye. She has to be wondering if this is my new boyfriend and if he sent the flowers. And ok, she's being a snoopy, but we keep an eye out for each other in this building.

I take the vase from her but have to set it on the floor while I unlock my door.

I can't thank you enough for accepting them for me, I thank her, they must have taken up a ton of room in your place.

She shrugs, —they smell really nice.

Once Danny and I and my flowers are all crowded into my living room I search for the mystery card. Not only is it sealed but my name and address are typed on the front.

Danny takes my suitcases into my bedroom, and I wonder if he's giving me little unnecessary privacy. I know he hasn't been dating anyone because I have a Darlene-spy in his department at work but he doesn't know the same about me. I want to reassure him because I seriously doubt they're from some secret admirer.

I have nothing to hide from you, assure him.

He doesn't say a word; he just shrugs and carries my stuff away.

He returns to find me sitting on the floor next to the vase, apparently confused.

Who they from, the card and the flower?

Joel Rockhurst. I say.

Joel Rockhurst? As in the CEO of JetStream, Joel Rockhurst?

Yeah, I nod still studying the card, —And it's handwritten. I think it's actually his handwriting. I hold it up for Danny to see.

What's it says?

Bob told me why you left the conference early, I read out the writing loud. I'm sorry for your loss. You and your father are an important part of the JetStream family, and it's signed by him for sure; I know his signature.

I didn't know Joel Rockhurst knew who your dad was, I don't think I've ever seen him down on the maintenance floor.

He didn't know who I was until recently when I got an iced tea for him during the golf tournament. I study the gorgeous, fragrant flowers, —The man must really like iced tea. I put the arrangement on my kitchen table where it takes up so much room I'll have to move it to eat. I put it on the coffee table, it blocks the TV screen, my already tight living Quarters just got that much more crowded.

That night, Danny doesn't stay in my apartment nor did he sleep with me in my apartment the next night or the rest of the week. I talk to him on the phone or we text but only because I'm contacting him about the storage garage we are renting together. He's putting distance between us and it feels awful. He's still hasn't given me a direct answer on moving in so I'm going to take that as a yes and move ahead with the plan. I offer to meet him at his place on Saturday morning so we can start packing, he reluctantly agrees.

When he opens the front door I want to jump into his arms and take a week's worth of sexual frustration out on him. He hugs me but stops there. The lack of kisses is unnerving and I'm not sure how to react. I try to keep things upbeat and make myself useful.

I follow him around with my iPad as he points out the few things he's taking with him and what needs to go into storage. I make notes about the number of boxes we will need and sizes. I also start a separate section on repairs and sprucing up that will need to happen before his house goes on the market.

When we reach his bedroom he stops the tour and finally asks. What are you working on there?

Just taking notes.

Notes about what?

Packing, painting, stuff like that.

Vivey, I got this, if you want to help a little fine, but I know what I'm doing.

I minimise my notes but don't delete them. Ok, what do you want me to do?

He looks around, and it's clear he doesn't really have a plan, I bite my tongue and wait for his instruction.

I guess start in the kitchen, pack stuff up in there.

OK, where are the boxes and packing supplies?

The boxes are in the garage if that's what you mean by packing supplies.

The tension has started building between us already but the idea of just throwing breakables in a box is too ludicrous for me not to challenge.

Do you have some bubble wrap or old newspaper I can use to protect stuff?

He lets out a deep sigh as he puts his hands on his hips, his stance that says he is struggling to be patient, but I'm not sure if it's with himself or me. I assume he doesn't have anything but boxes when he says. Fine, start in the extra bedroom and I'll see about finding some newspapers.

I back out of the room to avoid pushing up against him because he's irritated. My eyes linger on his bed, the one I seriously doubt we will be using today if things keep going like this.

I make a ton of progress in the room that used to belong to his son, the fact that it's full of extra stuff now tells me that his ex hasn't allowed visitation in Savannah and Danny has had to drive to see Nick for a while now.

As I sort through boxes of high school yearbooks and sports trophies, it hits me how little I really know about his past and the things that matter to him. I've memorized every detail I've been able to observe since I've known him but he's never really sat down and talked about his past to me. If I throw away, this plaque he got for volunteer work in high school, would it matter to him? It's from Habitat for Humanity and it shows that he can build, I didn't even know that he knew how to build a house.

Working in separate rooms is good for us because it helps dissipates the tension and he seems grateful when I offer to go get more boxes and pick up some sub sandwiches for lunch. Of course, I also grab bubble wrap, shrink wrap, packing tape and labels from the store and then sandwiches, chips, a six pack of his favorite beer and a bag of his favorite cookies. I toss a box of condoms in the cart before I check out, I can never be too prepared, you know?

I try to be subtle as I bring all of the packing supplies into the house and he doesn't mention them but glares to make sure I know he thinks I've gone overboard, and they're unnecessary. When it is lunch time, I use that opportunity to ask him a little more about his past.

I didn't know you could do carpentry.

He seems perplexed for a minute then remembers the plaque. Yeah, my family was big on doing charity work. Everybody had to do something. Building houses sounded easy to me.

This is the first time he's ever telling me about his family. You grew up in Florida, right?

He nods as he takes a bite of his sandwich.

Any brothers? Sisters?

He drinks some beer before answering, One brother.

Is he still in Florida?

He doesn't look at me and concentrates on tearing open a bag of chips as he says. No, he died. We were both in the military, he was stationed in Iraq. He didn't make it back.

My heart sinks and my throat is too tight to swallow another bite of food. I'm sorry, that's horrible.

Comes with the job, he says and shrugs.

I don't know why he's being so cavalier; if he never talks about it to anyone or if he is avoiding opening up specifically to me. I feel the same sting of distance I've been feeling all week from him. He's letting me into his life but only so far, only as much as he deems acceptable before he leaves.

I concentrate on my sandwich and wonder if maybe he's seeing this all so much more clearly than I am and he's right. Maybe we should just let New Orleans be a brief fling that we had and I should stop pushing him so hard. But the doubts in my mind are quickly whisked away by the truth I feel from my gut. We have a chance for something great here, even for a short time and I won't give up on it that easily. The carpe diem in my soul is a final gift from my dad and I can't ignore it.

I change the subject. —Have you ever watched any shows about staging?

Like building sets for a play? He shakes his head.

No, staging is setting a house up to sell faster at the best price. Really?

Yeah, they have all these shows about what paint colors to choose and how to arrange the furniture and do things to make buyers see it as their home.

Let me guess, you've watched them all, he says, and I believe it's true, he's being obtuse, pretending not to know why I brought this up.

I've watched a few, I mean I've already got some great ideas that we could do really cheaply; a little paint, some flowering plants, I've seen them use spray paint to make old appliances look amazing.

And the patronizing glare is back.

I'm just trying to help.

But again, he pushes me away. I know you are but it's not necessary. You helping me pack some of this stuff up is enough. He might be trying to tell me that my help will not be needed after today, but I can play at the obtuse game too. I will keep doing it, keep showing up and helping until he admits how much he needs me, it's for his good and mine.

CHAPTER FOURTEEN

I pack boxes all day on Saturday and when the sun sets, he offers to take me to dinner as a thank you. It's a sweet gesture and one I hope will lead to more romance, but I can feel that it's also his way of evening out the score and letting me know he will do the rest himself.

Our conversation at dinner is neutral, Savannah news and weather, but I touch him a lot and he starts to loosen up. He holds my hand as we leave the restaurant. He puts his arm across my shoulders and pulls me close when we're blasted by a chilly breeze. There's a spark there, I can feel it, but unlike him, I can't turn it off.

Back at his place, parked in his driveway he hesitates. We sit in silence and I feel like he's waiting for me to do something but I don't know what. Is he waiting for me to announce that I'm going home? Because that's not happening. I can feel his reluctance but it only makes me want to work harder, to show him how great we could be together.

He finally opens his door and asks. You coming in? It's not exactly seduction but I'll take it.

Things are no less strained inside. He seems lost amid the sea of boxes. He doesn't offer, so I don't take off my jacket. Instead I stand in the foyer waiting for his next move.

Thanks for your help today, he says and looks around, acknowledging all our hard work.

Not a problem. I can help tomorrow too. As in, why don't I spend the night, and we can get back to work tomorrow. I hope he gets the hint because it's about as forward as I can get with him. Will I ever be able to completely relax when we are together?

He catches my hint but doesn't grab on. Vivey, he takes my hand and studies it as he rubs his thumb across it. His tone is gentle for his brush-off. I shouldn't have let things get to this point, you know, I'm sorry.

I try to make things lighter. What? Me helping you pack?

He replies with his standard glare. —Us sleeping together, New Orleans was... He struggles to find the words. I wait with tension building up in me, I'm pensive, and fear has cloud my thoughts. —We were both hurting, needed each other, but.

I can't let him do this, I won't let him finish dismissing me from his life. I grab on to a final thread. Fine, my voice cracks with my lie. It's not fine but I have to pretend it is if I want to stay in his life. We can go back to being friends, friends help each other move.

He looks up and shakes his head, possibly pleading for help from my dad to win this argument with me. That's just it, I don't want to just be friends. I feel great when I'm with you, but there is nowhere for this to go. When he looks at me, he sees the hope in my eyes. The only thing I heard was that he feels great when we are together. Anything after that was lost to me.

He stares at me and says, I'm leaving and there's no way around it, Vivey.

So let's feel great together until you do, I immediately, using his words against him but leave off until I figure out another plan. I lean onto him, terrified that he will push me back.

He doesn't, it takes him few seconds before he hugs me back and kisses me.

I'm winning as I get instant flood or combination of lust and emotion. I peel off my jacket and toss it on the floor then reach for his. I know he said he likes to be in charge during sex but I have to be right now. He didn't know that he gave me ammo when he said that he likes having sex with me and I'm using the ammo to my advantage now.

I get entangled in the kiss while I pour every bit of emotion I've got into the kiss as I pull my shirt up. I stop kissing him and press myself against him while I pull my shirt up. Realising that he is not responding as much as I respond to the romance, I unhook my bra and let it fall between us. My breats hangs firm before him, and immediately I see his eyes trail down toward them. He slowly reaches down and puts a warm hand over one and I know I've got him just as much as he's got me while we both moan with pleasure.

I feel powerful and sexy. I grab the hem of his shirt and push it up until he has to lift his arms so I can get it over his head. I wrap my arms around his neck and graze my nipples against his warm skin and the hair on his chest. I can't imagine how he's not feeling the same white-hot need that I am, but I still feel his indecision.

I kiss him again, letting him feel my desire, and then I whisper, — Make me feel good. My voice is muted by my heavy breathing. —Let me make you feel good, and please, please do not turn me down now because I can't take it.

My pleading is his undoing. He pulls me in tight bends his knees slightly, then stands and lifts me with him as he moves toward the bedroom. Yes! Oh, God yes! I might come just from the thrill of victory. I've just succeeded in seducing the man of my dreams.

But my victory is short lived. He's on board but determined to take over. He can't let me win and have my way. He tosses me on the bed and I reach for him but he backs away. He sits on the end of the bed, too far away for me to touch him, but close enough that I can see what he's doing. He leans down and unties his shoe before pulling it off.

Then he does the same to the other. It's a painfully slow process that has me squirming with frustration as I feel my passion starting to cool. I reach for the button on my jeans but he reaches around and stops me. He places my arms above my head one by one, not speaking but also not bothering to hide his agenda. It kills me but I stay put. I lay there and watch as he continues to slowly undress.

It's one hell of a show with a finale that has my mouth watering but I hate only being allowed to be the audience. I keep my hands where he put them but I clench my fingers and pop my knuckles in frustration. He goes into his bathroom and I can hear him opening and closing now empty drawers. He has to be looking for his stash of condoms.

I moved them to your top dresser drawer, I call from the bed.

He doesn't respond, he comes out of the bathroom and stares at me for reading his mind and being right. What was I supposed to do, wait for him to rifle through every box in the room? I think aloud, and I keep my hands in place but stare back at him. Excuse me for solving your problem.

He tosses a string of three wrapped condoms on the night stand, I smile up at him. Three? I smirk and wink at him.

He laughs, Yes, three, if you're lucky.

He lays down next to me and pulls me to him, I wrap my arms around his neck. His look reminds me that that they are not where he wants them.

They were falling asleep, I lie.

He studies my face, and I feel like a child caught lying, probably because I am.

Don't you trust me?

No, he replies me.

I flinch and he softens the reply by kissing me sensually and then lays down the rules for the night.

You want me to make you feel good and I want to and I will, but I don't want to fight you or have to second guess your every move. He pushes the hair off my neck and kisses me where he knows I love it. Relax, can you do that for me?

I nod my agreement even though I'm seriously questioning my ability to do it.

Relaxing is a foreign concept to me. Surrendering is the antithesis of my being.

CHAPTER FIFTEEN

We uses two of the condoms that night and the third in the morning. I definitely won't say the sex was bad, far from it, but just like our relationship, it was intense. One night with Danny is an opus, there's lust and power struggles that end in blessed release followed by regret (his), tears (mine) and finally tenderness. I initiate morning sex, taking advantage of his morning wood. I won't say he was mad when he's awake enough to realize my plan, but the sex that follows was rough and Quick and he might have hoped one-sided. But I love it. Maybe because it's Danny and I lust him, but more likely because it's Danny and I want all of him, even his frustration and anger

The weekend goes with the lust and intense sex we both had and now are both ready for a few days apart, away from each other. It's not like he isn't on my mind most of the time, I do think about him but in my quiet hours alone in my apartment my brain does what it always does; organizes, I create a color-coded and timeline/work chart. I painstakingly research how long it will take to do each task to make his house more marketable, then schedule them in the most efficient order and assign them. I print out two copies to take with me on Friday night when he's said I can come over again.

My efforts are not appreciated as we fight over it from day one.

I call Dom every morning on my ride to work so she can help me analyse everything going on between me and Danny.

We're fighting about the paint again.

Jeeeezus, not the paint again, she exclaims. Is he still mad you made him take that first color back? Dom must have her own flow chart on her white board to keep track of all our issues.

Probably. Last night he took his bed apart and scraped the walls up as he carried it through the living room.

Which is why you wanted to paint it last, she concurs, thank God I have Dom who understands the perfect logic of my plan.

I know, I had to literally bite my lip and leave the room to keep from yelling, I told you so. But he knew, I didn't have to say it and ow I have to paint that same goddamned wall all over again. Third time!

These talks are supposed to calm me down, but I'm getting all riled up again, nothing grates on me more than gross inefficiency. —He fights me on everything. It's like he hates me now.

He doesn't hate you, you fight, then you get to make up...lots of make-up sex, right?

I'm suddenly silent, I don't reply because even our sex life is starting to reduce, too.

Not so much, I admit.

Oh, she says which tells me that even Dom is running out of answers.

I'm secretly thrilled when he dismantles his bedroom because it means he can start to stay at my place. I reason that maybe things will be better if we are away from the things we keep fighting about, but it turns out to be another grudging compromise. Some nights, he comes home with me, without a suitcase or even his toothbrush, which means now sex and it affects our sex life pretty much.

The passion is gone, even the angry passion. I'm starting to feel like sex is now just another task on our color-coded timeline.

One night after a particularly ugly fight about how to arrange things in the storage unit, he lay in bed next to me but felt a million miles away already. I want to apologize but don't because I feel I'm right, damn it. But I also want to try to grasp at his love that I can feel rapidly pulling away from me.

Arrange the locker any way you want, I say. It's not an apology but a concession.

He breathes a heavy sigh. —I don't care about the goddamn locker, and you're right anyway. The last sentence sounds completely defeated.

Danny I.I begin to explain my position again but he cuts me off.

You're right, Ok? I've realize it, goddamnit! You're right about the paint and the furniture and the fact I need to take vitamins, you're right about the realtor and that I need to buy new work boots. You are right about everything.

I just want to help you, I shrug and squeak out. I have a horrible tightness in my chest that I'm having trouble talking through. It's the words I've been dying to hear but not in his demoralised tone.

He lies back with a sigh, I know you do, Vivey, I know. He stares at the ceiling and I wait for the but-statement that will follow.

What? Say it. Whatever it is.

Don't wait for me.

I bite my lip and look down so he can't read my face, I'm caught. It's clear that he is leaving and I have been planning our lives secretly once he returns, but he doesn't know about it.

I have a three year contract, do not wait for me, he says stresses each word.

I don't answer because I won't agree to something I had no intention of doing.

He catches my lack of answer. Fuck, slips out before he can stop it. He rubs his forehead as if I'm giving him a headache. —We never should have started this.

I cry and sniff without facing him; I can't face him now until he looks at me.

Vivey. He brushes the tears away from one cheek as I wipe them from the other. Vivey, I know you're not going to understand this but I love you, I swear I do, but that's why I need you to agree not to wait for me.

That makes no sense, I sniff again and try to curtail my crying. If you love me then we should be together.

No. He reaches over and pulls me to him. No, it doesn't mean we should be together. In our case, it means we should let go before we kill each other.

He settles me against his chest. Vivey, isn't it obvious now that I'm not the right guy for you? I don't want you wasting three years of your life not meeting the guy who is right for you.

Is this because I'm pushy? I ask him crying, I don't know if he can read the terror in my voice, but I'm naming my biggest fear; that it's because of me, of who I am, that we failed.

He breathes out and carefully chooses his words, I have never met anyone who needs others less than you. He turns on the pillow to look at me. I need to be needed, Vivey. I want to be needed, I want to be right sometimes.

I'm crying hard now because this really is the end of us, the end of my Danny dream, we tried, and I failed.

I have no counter arguments because for once he's right. I don't need anyone, even him, I curl up against him and let him hold me while I cry myself to sleep.

CHAPTER SIXTEEN

You know that sick feeling you get when you are still technically in a relationship, but you know it's really already over? Danny and I are still a couple, but...

He goes to Charlotte to visit his son for Christmas while I'm at Dom's trying not to spread my desolation all over her family gathering. Luis's family is there, too, doubling the number of people that are supposed to be around. I hide out in Dom's room a lot, pretending to not obsessively check my phone for calls or texts from Danny.

I make an appearance at dinner but wish it was socially appropriate to eat alone in the kitchen. I put up sham smiles often times, which I'm not sure if anyone else is buying, but Dom isn't. She corners me in her room and lures me out of my cone of sadness with her aunt's killer pie.

I'm glad you're here.

Seriously? I smirk. I don't think I'm really adding to the festivities.

I would be worried sick about you if you weren't here.

I lay my head on her shoulder and take another bite of pie. Thank you. You don't need to worry about me, but thank you.

I do worry about you because here's the thing: you think you're Wonder

Woman, and you are probably the closest thing alive to her, but you're still human, and you've had the shit kicked out of you these past few months.

Even Wonder Woman gets to lean on her sidekick.

She didn't have one.

What? What about Steve Trevor?

I laugh a little and shake my head at her ironic mistake. Boyfriend and no, theirs was not a cry-on-my-shoulder kind of relationship. I soothe my raw emotions with another huge bite of pie. I thought I wanted Danny but I guess I only wanted the idea of Danny. He was right about one thing; we sucked as a couple.

I thought I wanted my dad to butt out of my life, I shake my head at the memories of all the times I told him to back off and pull in another shaky breath. Now he has.

You didn't make that happen; you are not that fucking powerful, she counters and hugs me to her, rubbing my back while at it, and I'm here for you, I'm not going anywhere.

You're getting married, sweetie, I point out. Luis will have you and you'll have him. I lie back on the bed and set my empty plate on Dom's side table. I stare at the posters on the ceiling of her bedroom as I've done a thousand times before and contemplate my life. My problem is that I want a guy, but I don't.

No, you want a man, but you don't need one.

I always thought that was a good thing.

Dom lies down next to me and grabs my hand. It is and you'll see, I promise. There will be someone, a smoking hot male someone, who can handle you, deal with how amazing you are; someone who will appreciate you.

I'm glad you're so sure.

Are you going to his going away party?

I shrug, maintenance is having a happy hour get together at The Rail to send Danny off to the land of no liquor or unmarried women. I'll probably stop by but Bob's leaving for a major sales presentation in

Seoul the next day. I need to be at work early to make sure he has everything.

I'll go with you if you want.

I give her hand a squeeze but don't reply because for once I'm not making plans.

My life feels too unstable and uncertain to plan even a few days ahead...except for work.

God bless my job.

I do stop by Danny's going away party, briefly and alone. Part of me wants to see everyone from maintenance, especially Darlene, and to be honest, part of me wants to see how Danny acts toward me around them.

If I need a final message that we are officially not a couple, I get it. He gives me a quick, friendly hug when I get there then moves on to make the rounds and talk to his friends. I don't think anyone else notices, but Darlene does. She comes over and stands next to me.

Wanna talk?

I shake my head.

She studies me for a moment. You knew he was leaving, right?

I nod.

Hurts anyway?

I nod again and she puts her arm around me squeezing it a bit. Call me anytime you need to talk, OK?

I give her a weak nod, — Thanks then stands next to her for what I hope is an appropriate amount of time before I beat it out of there. I wave to Darlene before I leave but don't look back at Danny.

The next day I have Bob packed up and in the air before noon. He's taking one of our newest, largest jets to demo for a Korean investor. As I stand watching him take off from runway nineteen I glance across at the commercial terminal. Danny's there right now. I check the time on my phone. He's probably waiting to board his flight to New York where he'll connect with his flight to Riyadh.

I left him a note this morning, telling him good bye. Telling him that I love him and probably still will when he comes back, whether he likes it or not.

He still has a half hour until boarding. It would take me at least forty- five minutes to drive to the other side of the airport. Or... I could use the security clearance I keep for moving Bob's stuff around and take the direct route.

I commandeer one of the linemen from the JetStream ramp and asked him to give me a ride across. I have him drop me near Danny's gate. I've never abused my clearance before, and can't believe I'm doing it now, but I submitted to everything short of an anal probe to get the security badge that I'm now flashing all over concourse C. I deserve to use it illicitly at least one time.

Danny doesn't look overly surprised when he sees me approaching. He smiles a little and nods. Of course, you know how to get in here without a ticket.

I flash my badge at him. Of course.

I'm not exactly sure what I came to say but I want us to part on a better note. We stand in an uncomfortable silence for a few minutes. He doesn't look at me, but finally speaks.

You are amazing. You know that, right?

I want to say, —But not amazing enough for you? But that would keep us in the same place we had been for weeks now. So I say thank you instead.

I touch his hand and he takes mine. I know you don't see it, but you are still the most amazing man I have ever known.

He chuckles. Then you must have not gotten to know me too well, He squeezes my hand, —I'm still going to check up on you, you know. I'll be home once a year. He looks out the window at the

JetStream headquarters across the field. I expect you'll be running the place by the time I'm back.

I chuckle. —I run Bob's life. That's enough for me.

You say that, but, he shakes his head. No, you are going to go incredibly far Vivey; way too far for a grease-monkey like me.

I don't agree with him.

They call final boarding for his flight and when he bends down to grab the handle of his carry-on, I let go of his hand. He leans in and gives me a quick kiss on the lips before he turns to go.

I call after him, — Love you. I don't know if he heard me or not but he doesn't turn around again. I want to watch him board and watch his plane take off, hang on to him until he's out of the same airspace as me but my ride's waiting on the ramp.

I decide to take an afternoon off. Something I could do anytime Bob is out of town, but I never do. I'm in no mood for friendly office chatter today. I'm going home to sit on my perfect, oversized, tufted sofa and hug my pink chenille pillow. I need to dig my pristine linen sheets out of storage and put them back on the bed, my bed. I'm going to have to face it alone sometime, feel the silence, move around without Danny in my way, and miss him. I need time to grieve losing Danny and my dad.

I stop by my desk to pick up a few things when an urgent email catches my eye.

It's from Carolyn Guage, Joel Rockhurst's secretary. I open it.

Vivienne, I've set up a lunch meeting for you and Mr Rockhurst in his office Monday at 12:45. Please reply and confirm your attendance.

What the hell? Lunch for me and Joel Rockhurst? This has to be a mistake. I call Carolyn.

This is for Bob, right? He's out of town, but he'll be back late next week. We can reschedule it.

No. He specifically asked me to set up a lunch with you. —Why?

Don't know and he didn't offer a reason. You'll be here though? She posed it as a question, but everyone at JetStream knows that a request from Joel Rockhurst is really a command. No one tells him no.

Uh, sure. I'll be there.

Great. See you then.

I have no idea why he would want to have lunch with me but I'm sure my brain will come up with a few million between now and 12:45 on Monday. Whatever it is, my gut tells me this can't be good. I need to prepare to meet with the CEO but how do you prepare for the most random mystery meeting in the history of JetStream aerospace?

I call Dom.

THE END

9 781999 302382